THE Christmas Tree CORPSE

THE FOUR SEASONS BOOK TWO · WINTER

THE Christmas Tree CORPSE

RANDOLPH CREW

ARTEC

The *Christmas Tree Corpse*

Book two in the *Four Seasons* series
A Nate and Superman cozy murder mystery

Copyright © 2022 by Randolph Crew
Published by Artec Publishing

ISBN# 978-0-9651430-3-5
e-book ISBN# 978-0-9651430-2-8
PCN# 0-9651430-3-1

Edited by Marcia Ford
Copy edited by Elizabeth Smith
Cover design by Roseanna White Designs

Printed in the United States of America
First paperback edition: October 2022
First Kindle edition: October 2022

For Harper, my well-read granddaughter

Table of Contents

Prologue

My name is Nathan B. Hawke. I'm from Dallas, Texas, and for thirty-seven years I solved murders. While my career as a homicide detective may have officially started in Dallas, it actually began when I was in junior high school in Southern Pines, North Carolina. I had a reputation in those days that inhibited my crime-scene credibility, but...Well, let me explain it this way: From the fall of 1955 through the summer of 1956, I came across four dead bodies. None of them had died by any act of God; none had been washed up by a tsunami or zapped by lightning. They were murdered. When the local police wouldn't act on my information (that credibility thing), I tried to solve the murders myself. That's when my murder-solving career began.

I'm retired now, and I want to tell you about all four of those murders in a series of books called the *Four Seasons* series. In this second book, and again from my perspective at the time, I'll tell you about the body my dog and I found just before Christmas 1955. I call this one the case of *The Christmas Tree Corpse*.

Chapter 1

THE CORPSE

Christmas that year was on Sunday, but this story starts the weekend before Christmas, exactly a week before Christmas Eve and four days before school let out for our two-week Christmas vacation. That Saturday morning, under an overcast sky with a chill in the air, I waited outside our backdoor in my baseball cap and tan windbreaker. Mom and my sister Becky still hadn't gotten their act together, and Granddaddy was holed up in his workshop in our one-car garage. The mission that morning was to buy a Christmas tree. The gray sky and chill in the air only hinted at the emotional chill we'd get at that tree farm.

Superman waited patiently beside me while I ran some fresh water for him from the faucet by the backdoor. Believe it or not, that dog had a cowlick just like mine, but his was tan while mine was sandy blond, at least at that time in my life it was sandy blond. I turned off the water and heard the crunch of gravel from our two-lane driveway.

Charlie, my broad-shouldered, hawk-nosed friend and descendant of an Osage chief on his father's side, wheeled his bike between the back bumper of our sky blue '52 Ford and the corner of our two-bedroom brick house. He slammed on the brakes and slid to a stop in our backyard.

In the age of crew cuts and buzz cuts, Charlie wore his brown hair ear-hole long and parted down the middle. He pushed his hair out of his eyes and over his ears, then dismounted and popped his kickstand into place. He walked toward me with his hands in the pockets of his faded denim jacket.

"Hey, Nate, are we going today, or what? You said you'd call."

Superman jogged over to him with a bounce in his step and a hearty tail wag. Charlie paused a second to pat him on the shoulder.

I set Superman's water bowl on the deck of his "Superman suite," the chain-link U-shaped pen built against the brick wall of the house, then looked up.

"I said I'd call when *we* were ready, but, unfortunately, *we* are not ready yet."

Charlie scoffed. "Bossy Becky again?"

"Yep. Mom insisted Becky go with us—family time, you understand—so we wait."

Meanwhile, Superman looked up at Charlie with his beady eyes like, *That's it? One pat on my shoulder?*

Charlie ignored him and looked at me.

"Hey, you want to come over and see our tree when we get back? We finished it this morning, and I got to add the finishing touch, the 'la touché finale,' as my mother said."

"La touché? What's that? French? I thought your mother was from a line of Creek Indians."

He smiled. "She is, but it's the French-speaking branch of the tribe...in Paris."

"Paris? Come on, Charlie, I've never heard—"

"Okay, okay, just kidding. She was a language major in college, so she just likes to throw a little French phrase at us now and then."

"Yeah, well, I'd like to see your tree with that French doo-dad on top, but the way things are going here, it might be supper time by the time we get back. Hang on. I'll see if I can get this show on the road. You said this place was ten minutes away, right?"

"It was for us, but my dad's one of those 'enjoy the journey' types, so it might be more like five for your 'I'll race you there' mom."

I chuckled. "Yeah, probably. Be right back."

As I closed the backdoor to the kitchen, the door to the bedroom Mom shared with Becky must have opened because I heard Bing Crosby singing "White Christmas." Then Mom entered from the dining room wearing a bulky red-and-white sweater, jeans, and her leather booties.

"Well, Mom, is her highness finally ready?"

She pulled me aside and glanced back toward the dining room.

"Nate, do you know a guy named Gill, a tenth grader?"

"I ah...I think so. Plays football?"

"And basketball and baseball, and can probably bowl three hundred every game too."

"Yes, ma'am, I guess I know him, or I know of him."

"Well, what do you think?"

"What do you mean?"

"Is he okay?"

I shrugged. "I guess. You mean for Becky? Is she talking about this guy?"

"She sure is—nonstop. He smiled at her in the hall yesterday, and she still hasn't gotten over it."

"Well, I guess he's okay. At least he's better than that greaseball Vinnie she was in love with at Halloween."

I glanced back toward the dining room.

"Is that why we're running behind?"

"Yep. Apparently, Gill works at the tree farm we're going to. She's now into her fourth outfit and still can't decide what to wear."

"Well, Mom, Charlie's outside. He got tired of waiting for us, so he pedaled down here to see what was going on. Can't you get her in gear and get us on the road?"

"You're right." She turned toward the dining room. "We'll be out in a minute."

I opened the backdoor and found Charlie seated on the sundeck of the Superman suite with the beast himself lying flat on his back beside him. Superman, with his eyes half-closed, made low, guttural moans while Charlie rubbed his chest.

When I closed the backdoor, Superman turned his head and looked at me like, *Yes, sir—a cool drink, good companions, and a chest rub. I can dig it.*

"They'll be out in a minute, Charlie."

A crisp breeze hit me, so I stuffed my hands into the pockets of my jeans and leaned against the brick wall.

"Say, Charlie, did you ask your mom about driving us next Thursday night?"

"No, not yet. I keep hoping I'll get pneumonia or something and won't have to go."

"Well, if you do, give the bug to me, will ya? I'm not ready for this hold-hands-with-a-girl-and-dance thing, not even if it's Chipper's hand."

"Hey, who said you're the one that gets to dance with Chipper?"

"'Gets to?' Are you saying you want to dance with her? I thought you were going to be in bed with pneumonia."

He stood and Superman did a half-roll and popped to his feet.

"Well, if I don't get pneumonia and I have to dance with one of those Girl Scouts, I'd rather it be Chipper."

"Yeah, well, me too, but what if Susie Wilkerson latches onto you? I saw her crowding you in the lunch line yesterday. I think you're gonna have to sneak past her first."

"Is she a Girl Scout? I thought it was just Chipper, Rose, Donna, and the other usual suspects."

"Yep, she is. She may not be in Chipper's den or pack or whatever they call it, but she's in the same troop that's giving this party."

"Well, if she thinks she's gonna dance with me, she's crowding the wrong Tonto."

I heard the backdoor open and turned to see Mom step out, followed by Becky wearing Mom's red-plaid pencil skirt and her red pullover sweater. Mom was the secretary for the Southern Pines Police Department, and Becky was now wearing the same outfit Mom wore to the police department's Christmas party the weekend before. Since Becky was tall for her age, Mom's clothes fit her well, and they were seasonally appropriate, but in my humble opinion, they showed a little too much of her early blossoming. Mom didn't seem to disapprove, so we hopped into the car and drove toward the tree farm.

On the way, at ten miles per hour over the speed limit on a winding country road, Mom glanced at Becky in front, then at Charlie, Superman, and me in back.

"Now, kids, we've got to knock this out quickly, so don't dilly-dally around. Gunner has taken some Christmas vacation days, so I've got to go into the office this afternoon and pick up the slack."

Becky looked over at her. "Gunner?"

"Oh, sorry, I mean Officer Lum. His Korean name is Gun-woo, but he's been called 'Gunner' since his days with the military police. He told me Gun-woo means 'hope for mankind.'"

I poked Charlie, whose last name—Shonkasabe—means "Black Dog," then leaned over Superman and whispered, "Cool nickname, but not as cool as 'Black Dog.'"

Charlie leaned over to me.

"And a whole lot better than 'Cowlick.'"

I pushed him.

"Hey. You gonna call me that now?"

"Not me, Kemosabe. And I'll stomp anyone who does."

"Really? You gonna stomp Tom Ray?'"

"Eh. May need your help with that one."

Mom grinned at us in the rearview mirror. It always amazed me how good her ears were.

Ahead of us on the right side of the road, a four-by-eight sheet of plywood stood staked in the tall dead grass. In words scrawled in white paint as if a third grader had written them, it read Christmas Trees Ahead.

A few seconds later, we parked on the right side of the road behind four other cars and two pickup trucks. We got out and walked toward a row of fifteen to twenty Christmas trees leaning against the other side of a stacked split-rail fence. I held Superman on his leather leash, and we followed a family with four excited kids in overalls. In a light, crisp breeze and under a darkening sky, we entered through a gap in the fence and onto a cleared field of stumps.

To our left, at the head of the field and beside a rusty red pickup, a tall blond teenager in jeans and a blue varsity jacket hammered an X-shaped tree stand to a six-foot Christmas tree. A young, well-dressed couple stood behind the truck and watched while the woman cuddled a bundled-up, dark-haired baby. A sign against the back of the truck said the trees were eight, six, and four feet tall and cost a dollar a foot. A tree stand was two dollars.

Mom stopped us.

"A six-foot tree, guys. That's it." She looked at each of us in turn. "Becky, you pick one; Nate, you pick one, then I'll decide which one to buy."

Mom had been through this routine before and obviously didn't want a repeat of last year's loud arguments and near slug fest over which tree we would buy. They ended up siding against me.

I hustled past a tall, bearded man in a crumpled, sweat-stained fedora and a pair of faded bib overalls that struggled to contain his bulging stomach. He held a four-footer out to the couple with the four kids, spit a shot of tobacco juice over the top rail of the fence, then turned to the man.

"This is your tree, friend, ol' Jasper's best; I cut it this morning just for you."

Superman and I slowed as we passed a gray-haired couple looking at another four-footer, then we stopped at the row of six-footers. Mom and Charlie walked up beside us. Becky walked past us and beyond a couple with two brown-haired little boys in matching plaid jackets and caps. The man stood the first eight-footer on its stump, and the boys hopped around it and fluffed the limbs. Becky stopped at the last eight-foot-er—the one closest to the rusty pickup and the stud in the varsity jacket.

This was going to be easy! Becky was out of it!

Only three six-footers were left, and all three were scrag-gly with uneven limbs. Plus, they were like the shrubs around Charlie's house, not the classic Christmas tree I was hoping we'd buy. I looked at Charlie.

"These are tall shrubs, not Christmas trees."

"My father said they're Leyland cypress, the only Christ-mas tree types that grow well here in the Sandhills."

I looked at the field behind us and pointed.

"That's the kind of tree we got last year, Charlie. That's a Christmas tree."

"Yeah, those are Fraser firs, but they didn't do well this year—the mites got into 'em."

"Well, they look nice and green to me, and I see the one I want."

I pulled on Superman's leash.

"Come on, dog, let's go check it out."

While Mom walked up to where Becky was pretending to be interested in the last eight-footer in the lineup, Charlie, Superman, and I jogged over to the split-rail fence on the back side of the field. We hopped over the fence and stepped into the field with the real Christmas trees. That's when Superman pulled his leash tight and dragged me through the first row of trees and past the tree I had in mind.

Geez, not again!

"Stay, Superman, stay!"

But he didn't stay or stop until his bull terrier rump had followed his bloodhound nose right through the second row and to the third row, where he stopped at the base of a ten-foot Fraser fir.

Behind me, I heard, "Hey, git outta there! Hey, you kids, get back ovah heah."

I turned. Between the tops of the trees in the row of six-footers, I saw the Goliath in the crumpled fedora, 'ol' Jasper,' waddle to the split-rail fence we had just hopped over. He pointed at us.

"Hey, git back heah!"

Charlie, who had stopped at the first row, cupped his hands around his mouth.

"Nate, come back!"

I pulled on Superman's leash.

"Sorry, mister! My dog got away from me!"

I yanked the leash, but Superman dug in and didn't move.

He pulled his nose away from the tree and glanced at me like, *Got something here, boss. Gimme some slack.*

I could see something was there all right—something unnaturally long, thick, and lumpy. Partially hidden by overhanding green limbs and covered in cut branches, it curved around the tree trunk and rested on the bottom row of branches in a space where two rows of branches had been cut away. But so what? It was none of my business.

I took a step closer and yanked the leash again.

"Come on, Superman, get away from—"

And that's when a burst of cold wind whistled through the trees and blew away one of the cut limbs. I did a double take.

I looked over my shoulder to yell at Charlie to join me, but he had already hopped back over the fence.

Ol' Jasper stood beside him.

"Git back ovah heah, kid, or I'll come ovah there and drag you back!"

I watched him try to get his gut over the fence, but by that time the famous Nathan Hawke curiosity thing had taken over.

I turned back to the tree, kneeled, then raised the row of limbs above the long, lumpy thing. A few dead needles rained on my windbreaker. I removed a few more cut limbs, then froze. The lumpy thing was something human-sized wrapped inside an old army blanket.

Superman wiggled in beside me and stuck his nose up through the bottom limbs.

I blew out a breath, hesitated, but then carefully removed the last cut limb.

The blanket had two chalk-white fingers sticking out the top of it.

I choked back a gag, but now in detective mode, I leaned over the blanket, got a whiff of liniment, then flicked the top finger—stiff, stiff as a nail.

A little unsteady, I pulled out, stood, then dragged Superman back to the split-rail fence.

Ol' Jasper, who had given up on getting his gut over the fence, waited for me. He crossed his arms over his overalls and stared down at me with violence in his cloudy blue eyes.

I looked up at him and pointed toward the tree with the rolled-up blanket in it.

"Mister…there's a dead body in that tree."

Chapter 2
THE LITTER CLUE

O l' Jasper put his hands on his hips and leaned into me.

"What'd you say?"

By that time, everyone in the field was walking toward us.

I squinched my nose from his onion breath and body odor and stabbed a finger at the tree.

"I said there's a dead body in that tree!"

He shook his head and spit a shot of tobacco juice that splattered in the dirt beside my Converse high-tops.

"Sure, kid, a body in that tree. Get your butt back over heah!"

He reached over to grab me, but Mom, who had just stepped up beside him, slapped his arm down and pushed him aside.

"Come on, Nate, get back over here and tell me what's going on."

The guy looked down at her and raised his hands as if to push her back, but the crowd had gathered around him, so he apparently thought better of it and backed off.

As Superman and I hopped over the fence, Becky and the varsity stud jogged up beside Mom. Becky pointed at me.

"That's my stupid brother, Gill, and he's lying again. I can tell."

Granted, I did have that reputation, but Mom and I had an understanding about that.

"I'm not lying, Mom. Honest. There's either a body or body parts wrapped in an army blanket and stuck in that tree over there."

She believed me and drove straight to the SPPD where she told Chief McDonald about the body. Then she called Detective Dan Lewis, then the coroner.

Meanwhile, back by the fence, Charlie and I told Gill and Becky what we'd seen. A few minutes later, we walked with them toward the rusty red pickup and Gill's tree stand construction job. At the same time—as ordered by Mom—I kept an eye on the Fraser fir field to make sure no one messed with the crime scene.

As we walked, I noticed the crowd, who couldn't see the body through the first two rows of trees, had gone back to tree shopping. Ol' Jasper, with an occasional glance at me, was now taking cash from the family with the four children.

I tapped Gill on the arm and nodded toward them. (It wasn't polite to point at people; another little etiquette thing that Mammy, our deceased and much-loved grandmother-like housekeeper, had drilled into us.)

"Gill, who's the big guy with the beard?"

"Oh, that's Mr. Jasper Barnes. His brother, Mr. Junior Barnes, owns all these fields, including this little tree farm, and Mr. Jasper manages them. He's okay, just a little rough around the edges."

He nodded toward the Fraser fir field.

"Did you see anything else over there?"

"You mean like clues?"

"Yeah, any evidence-like stuff?"

"No, just fingers sticking out of a blanket."

Becky, on his other side, brushed up against him.

"Well, enough of that, Gill. Tell me more about that car you're saving for."

I grabbed his arm.

"By the way, what happened to the Fraser firs? I was really counting on one of those."

Becky leaned her head around Gill and shot me a look.

"Oh, they got infected with mites, so they'll have to be destroyed. Mr. Junior is going to burn the whole field as soon as all the Leyland cypress trees are sold, then bulldoze it and start over with more cypress."

He glanced at Becky and then back to me.

"At Becky's request, I saved you a six-footer."

Becky leaned around him again, raised her eyebrows, and gave me a sharp nod like, *And it's the one I picked out, smart guy!*

I ignored her and looked over at the fence along the road.

"Well, you're down to three eight-footers and six four-footers, so you should be out soon."

"Yeah, we usually sell out in a week, and we opened last Saturday. I expect the rest to be gone by tonight. I think he'd planned to burn the field tomorrow, but now...I don't know."

By then we were at the truck, but Charlie nudged me and nodded back toward the field like he wanted to talk. I excused us and followed Charlie back to the part of the fence we'd hopped over.

He stopped and pointed at the top rail.

"You didn't move this rail, did you?"

"No."

"Did you see Mr. Barnes move this rail?"

"No. Why?"

"I didn't either, and I pretty much kept an eye on him the whole time you were over in the Fraser firs."

"So?"

"So, look." He pointed to the end of the rail. "See how this flat spot is darker than the rest of the rail?"

"Yeah."

"Well, that dark spot shows where the rail had rested on the end of the rail under it and unexposed to the sun for a long time, but now that dark spot is on top of the rail under it."

"In other words, someone may have recently taken this fence apart to move a body into the fir tree field."

"Exactly."

We both heard the siren and looked toward the road.

Detective Lewis parked his white Nash patrol car, and the siren moaned to a stop. Dressed in gray slacks, a white shirt, and a blue field jacket, he shut the car door and walked toward us using his signature long-legged lope. He carried a black case and pulled his Sergeant Friday fedora down snugly over his close-cut red hair. I could have picked that man out of a New York crowd just by his walk alone.

Meanwhile, an old, black pickup truck that had apparently followed the siren pulled over to the side of the road and parked behind our car. Three men in dirty straw hats and worn bib overalls hopped out of the front seat. The men, who looked like they might have just come from a morning of hard work in a tobacco field, climbed into the truck's bed and sat on the rail like they were there to watch a football game. The oldest, a gray-headed man with bright teeth and a pleasant smile, handed out sandwiches from a paper sack. The other two, both younger, didn't speak or smile. I checked my Timex; it was 11:12 a.m.

Mom arrived minutes later, followed by our sixty-something Chief McDonald in his unwashed, food-stained blue uniform. Then the coroner arrived and backed his green Chevy station wagon across the cypress field to the fence separating the Fraser firs.

The sullen young men in the truck, their cheeks full of food, elbowed one another with each new arrival.

Over at the split-rail fence, Mom joined Charlie and me while we stood in the field of stumps beside the coroner's Chevy, and I directed Lewis and the coroner to the crime scene.

While Lewis roped off the scene with a thick cord, the chief, with his police cap off-center as usual, limped back and forth behind us and smoked one cigarette after another. We watched Lewis take photographs, do sketches, and make notes, but we couldn't see what he or the coroner was doing when they bent down.

After twenty minutes at the crime scene, Lewis helped

the lanky coroner in the wire-rimmed glasses carry the blanket-wrapped body to the fence, then over the fence and into the coroner's station wagon.

As the coroner, then the chief drove off, Lewis walked over to Mom, Charlie, Superman, and me. Mom put her hand on his arm.

"Dan, could you ID the body, or…was it even a full body?"

"Yeah, full body."

He rubbed his neck and motioned for her to step aside with him. She followed him into the field a few yards while Charlie, Superman, and I stood and watched. He said a few words, then Mom gasped and put her hands to her face.

She hung her head, and I heard her say, "No, no, not Gunner…please."

Lewis tightened his lips and nodded.

Mom whispered something through her hands.

Lewis shrugged. "Don't know yet."

He gave her a shoulder hug, they paused a minute, then he took her arm, and they walked back toward us.

Mom came straight to me, wiped her eyes, and hugged me.

I held her tight and whispered, "Officer Lum?"

She sniffled and nodded.

Now back in official mode, Lewis took a notepad and ballpoint pen from his jacket pocket and turned to Charlie, me, and Superman. He knew us well, so he got right to it.

"Nate, tell me what you were doing in that field and how you discovered the body."

Superman raised his head and stuck his jaw out at Lewis like, *Hey, I was the one who found the body!*

I told Lewis how Superman had sniffed out the body and how the bearded guy, Jasper Barnes, reacted.

Superman grunted like, *That's better.*

"Do you think he was normally upset over you being in the field or overly upset?"

"It seemed an overreaction to me, but I had just met the guy, so I don't know."

He looked at Charlie. "Charlie?"

"I'd say overreaction, but like Nate, I'd just met the guy."

He wrote on the pad, then looked at me again.

"Nate, did you notice anything else while you were over there?"

"I noticed the tree was oozing resin from where a couple of rows of limbs had been cut, and I noticed the chopped or sawed-off limbs were placed around the blanket like camou-flage. And now that I think about it, they did look sawed, not chopped."

"Yeah, I agree. I noticed that too. I also found, along with your footprints, a lot of big footprints around the tree that weren't around the other trees."

Charlie, the Osage warrior and tracker, leaned in.

"See any drag marks, like heels being dragged?"

"No, don't think so."

"Then they must have carried the body to the tree. Come on; I'll show you."

While Detective Lewis and Charlie walked toward the fence, I put Superman in the car. He wasn't happy about it and looked at me like, *Hey, I'm on this case too, you know.*

I scratched behind his ear a second to console him, and

then I jogged back to the Fraser fir fence. I got there as Charlie pointed to the fence section he had shown me.

Charlie tapped the spot on the top side of the rail.

"This is probably where they came in; this top rail has been turned over recently."

Lewis touched the spot.

"So it has, Charlie, so it has. Good catch."

I pointed into the field.

"Detective Lewis, what could you tell from the footprints? Other than the size."

Lewis grinned and stepped back.

"Now, wait a minute, boys. This is not your case, okay? Let me handle it."

"Yes, sir, we understand—your case. But the footprints I saw had smooth soles and looked like they were made by street shoes."

"No, they were patterned like—" He laughed. "Oh, no you don't, Nate. Nice try."

I shrugged. "Just trying to help."

"The only way you can help is if you hear or see anything related to this situation, let me know."

He pointed at me.

"But do not—do not—go looking for murderers. Understand?"

I looked at Charlie.

"Looking for murderers" is a focused statement and doesn't include looking for clues to finding murderers.

Charlie had a half smile like he knew what I was thinking.

I looked back at Detective Lewis.

"Yes, sir. We understand. We won't go looking for murderers."

Lewis cocked his head like that wasn't exactly the answer he was looking for, but he had to get back to work. He shook his head and walked toward Mr. Jasper, who was now taking cash from the father of the little boys in the plaid jackets. At the exit, the mother and the two boys dragged an eight-footer toward a blue, four-door Buick.

Charlie and I watched and listened from a discreet distance while Lewis talked with Mr. Jasper, who kept looking at his clodhoppers and fidgeting with the straps of his overalls. He also kept denying he knew anything about the body. Mom hung around Becky and Gill. I figured Gill would be interviewed next, so I turned to Charlie.

"Hey. I've got an idea. Let's go."

"Go where?"

"Back to the crime scene."

As I strolled back toward the Fraser fir fence, Charlie joined me, but his frown told me he wasn't happy about it.

He shook his head.

"I don't know what you have in mind, Nate, but I don't think it's a good idea to go messing around that crime scene."

I looked straight ahead.

"We're not going to mess around. I just wanna look at those footprints Lewis mentioned. But first, I want to look at the footprints good ol' Mr. Jasper left on this side of the fence."

I stopped at the fence and pointed at the ground.

"He stood right in here somewhere."

Charlie pointed at a drop of tobacco juice on the top rail of the fence and two feet to the left of where we stood. He stepped back, took a side step to his left, then pointed at the ground.

"Right here, Nate."

And sure enough, there were pronounced prints in the sandy clay soil where Mr. Jasper's clodhoppers had struggled to support his huge frame.

I checked my pockets, but I didn't have a pencil or paper. I looked at Charlie.

"Hey, do you happen to have a pencil or paper?"

Charlie stuck his hands in the pockets of his denim jacket, then his jeans.

"As a matter of fact..." He shrugged. "I do not."

"Well, me neither. I guess we'll just have to compare notes and memorize them."

I squatted and pointed at the prints.

"I see a worn pattern on the soles and the outside of the heels of both the left and right boot. What do you see, my faithful friend and noted Osage tracker?"

Charlie, who had squatted beside me, pointed at the toe area of the prints.

"I see that, plus, I see a small notch in the toe of the right boot like it had kicked something at one time or maybe several times."

"Yeah, good, I see that. Anything else?"

"Well, it looks like the right boot is a little more worn than the left one, so that would indicate the man who made these prints was right-handed; right-handed people tend to push off with their right foot, so it gets more wear."

I looked over at Mr. Jasper, who was still over by the red pickup and still occupied with Detective Lewis.

"That figures because I saw him raise that four-foot tree with his right hand—the tree he sold to the couple with the four kids." I stood. "Okay, let's go check out the prints around the tree."

"Really, Nate, let's wait for Detective Lewis. I mean, it's Mr. Jasper's field, so his prints are bound to be everywhere in there."

"Well, sure, but they shouldn't be concentrated around one tree. And fresh."

"Yeah, but..."

"Okay, stay here and let me know if anyone notices what we're doing. I'm going to look."

"Crap, Nate. One day that curiosity of yours will get you in deep doo-doo."

"Maybe it will; maybe it won't." I hopped over the fence. "Be right back."

I walked passed the first row of trees, the six-footers, and noticed the tree I originally had in mind was almost totally brown on the other side.

The second row was eight-footers. That's where I had to stop at the cord barrier left by Detective Lewis. I looked back at Charlie, who had moved a few feet to his right so he could peer between the tops of the trees and keep an eye on me.

The cord ran around a couple of eight-footers, then straight into the row of ten-footers and one tree down from the tree with the missing limbs. I stepped along the outside of the cord toward the ten-footers. I looked for footprints along the way, but the only prints I saw were from smooth-sole shoes, so they probably belonged to Detective Lewis or the coroner. When I got to the ten-footers, I got behind the one next to the tree with the missing limbs and ducked under the cord.

Still no other prints, but…there was a piece of paper, like a sandwich wrapper, wadded up and under a limb of the tree beside me. I squatted, reached in, picked it up, then held it under my nose. Ketchup and onions. And fresh. I slipped it into the pocket of my windbreaker.

"Nate!"

Crap, not now.

"Nate, get back here. Quick!"

I took a cautious step toward the scene and did a quick scan. There were footprints everywhere; if Mr. Jasper's were among them, I couldn't tell and didn't have time to look. I stepped back and under the cord.

"Coming!"

I went down a few trees and then cut back toward the fence. I popped out of the field just as Mom stopped beside Charlie.

Mom turned toward me, tilted her head, and gave me one of her "I know you've been up to something" looks.

I jumped the fence and walked toward her.

"You ready to go, Mom?"

"Yes, but what were you—"

I jerked my thumb over my shoulder.

"That tree I saw that looked good? Well, it wasn't—lots of

brown limbs on the other side, like mite damage. You need help with our tree, right?"

I motioned to Charlie.

"Come on, Charlie, let's strap that thing in the trunk and roll. I'm hungry."

"Nate…" Mom blew out an exasperated breath.

Charlie and I jogged toward the red pickup with Becky's six-foot tree in it, and as we jogged, Charlie glanced at me.

"You're too much; you know that? You can lie without lying. Amazing."

"I wasn't lying. I really did check out that tree."

"Yeah, and the crime scene. What'd you see?"

"Footprints everywhere. I hope Lewis's photos will show what it looked like before he and the coroner stomped around in there."

We slowed to a walk a few yards before we got to the truck. Becky had walked by us on her way to our car, but Gill was still by the truck with Detective Lewis.

Over by the fence along the road, Mr. Jasper stood with a woman in a double-breasted green coat who held the hand of a small child in a coat and cap. The child pulled on the limbs of one of the last two four-footers while Mr. Jasper rocked side to side and occasionally cast a wary eye over at us.

As we walked up to the truck, Lewis lowered his notepad.

"Okay, Gill. Thanks for your help. If I need to talk with you again, I'll give you a call."

He flipped his notepad closed and pocketed the pen and pad in his blue jacket. He stepped toward the exit, and as he passed us, he said, "See you later, boys."

THE CHRISTMAS TREE CORPSE

Gill walked around to the tailgate and dragged a tree out of the bed. He looked at me.

"Your mom said you had a tree stand."

"Oh yeah, we're good. Thanks."

I grabbed a bottom limb.

"Good to meet you, Gill. See you around school."

Charlie grabbed another bottom limb and pointed at Gill.

"And at the next basketball game."

"Okay, I'll look for you. And bring Becky. I need all the fans I can get."

We waved and dragged the tree, stump first, toward the exit.

I turned to Charlie and increased my pace.

"Let's catch up with Detective Lewis. I don't want him to get away before I find out a couple of things."

"Like what?"

"Like, did Gill tell him about the burn scheduled for to-morrow?"

As we hustled through the exit, the three football fans in the old black pickup truck pulled onto the road in a U-turn, then drove away. As they did, a white, scrunched-up paper flew over the open tailgate of the truck.

We stopped at the trunk of our car, which was already open, and dropped the tree.

"Charlie, quick, go stop Detective Lewis. I'll be right there."

I checked for traffic, then ran onto the road and scooped up the paper.

Mom hollered from the driver's seat of our car, "Nate, get out of the road!"

As I jogged past her, I waved and continued to Lewis's SPPD patrol car. The engine was running, but Lewis had his arm on the open window sill, and Charlie stood by the side-view mirror and spotlight.

Lewis turned his head, smiled, and said, "Okay, Nate, what is it?"

"Phew! Well, first of all, let me check the paper I just took out of the road."

"Yeah, I noticed that. Very civic-minded of you to be so litter conscious."

I took the wrapper from my windbreaker pocket—the one I'd found under the tree—and compared it with the one from the road. Both smelled the same, like ketchup and onion, and had grease stains. With my right hand, I held the first one by a corner and showed it to Lewis.

"I found this under a tree near the crime scene."

With my left hand, I held up the other in the same way.

"This one flew out of the back of that black pickup that just pulled away."

"Well, Nate..." He shrugged. "They look like hamburger wrappers from Benny's Diner to me. What's your point? Are you thinking fingerprints?"

"Yes, sir, prints. If the prints on the wrapper I found under the tree are not Mr. Jasper's or anyone who works at the tree farm, they might be from the killer or killers."

"Yeah, that makes sense."

"And if the prints from the wrapper that just flew out of

that truck match prints from the wrapper under the tree, then whoever ate that burger could be the killer."

He chuckled. "Or they drove by here yesterday, and a wrapper flew out of their truck, and the wind blew it into the field of trees."

"Okay, Nate." He pulled the pen out of his pocket. "I'll mark them and hang onto them for now. How about that?"

I could tell he wasn't fully on board, but at least he wasn't ruling it out.

"Yes, sir. Thanks. Oh, and don't forget: Killers always return to the scene of the crime."

He chuckled. "Yeah, that happens."

As he wrote in the corner of each wrapper, I added, "What did Gill have to say?" (I always found it best to ask open-ended questions.)

"Nothing, really. He didn't know how the body could have gotten there; he hadn't been in that field; he hadn't seen anyone in that field lately."

"So, he didn't tell you they plan to burn that Fraser fir field tomorrow?"

He looked up and leaned back.

"No, he didn't. You know that for a fact?"

"I know that's what he told us." I looked at Charlie. "Right, Charlie?"

"Yes, sir. That's what he told us. He said they would burn the field to kill the mites after they sold the cypress trees, and they expected to sell them by tonight."

Lewis took out his notepad.

"So, they sell out tonight and burn tomorrow."

Charlie and I said in unison, "Yes, sir."

Lewis scratched the red stubble on his chin.

"That could explain why I caught Mr. Barnes talking to Gill right before I walked up to interview him. Barnes did look anxious to say his piece and get away from Gill before I got there."

Charlie looked at me. "Kinda disappointed in Gill."

"Yeah, me too."

"Well, boys, don't condemn Gill just yet. We don't know what was said; plus, we don't know if Gill figured the crime scene was already established and the burn wouldn't happen. In that case, mentioning it wasn't necessary. For now, Let's give him the benefit of the doubt."

He put his notepad and pen back in his pocket.

"But I'd better remind Mr. Barnes that the field is off limits for everyone and is not to be touched until I say so."

Lewis switched off the engine, got out of his car, then walked toward Barnes, who had the last four-footer in his hand and was waddling toward the red truck. A middle-aged couple in jeans and barn coats followed him while Gill waited for them with a new tree stand.

As Charlie and I finished loading our tree into the trunk, I said, "Did you recognize anyone in that old black pickup parked behind us—the one that just left?"

"Yeah, now that you mention it, I believe I did. I think I've seen them and their truck in front of our neighbor's house. They were trimming shrubs, removing shrubs, and planting other shrubs, so I guess they're in the landscaping business."

I tied off the end of a length of cord to the trunk latch and then looped the other end of the cord around the bumper. I pulled the trunk lid tight against the tree and looked up at Charlie.

"I wonder if that landscaping business includes trimming rows of limbs off the inside of a Fraser fir."

Chapter 3

NOT HAPPY

That night, as we ate supper in the dining room, Mom asked Becky and me about school, then she talked about decorating the tree after supper. She seemed over the shock of Officer Lum's death, so as Nat King Cole sang, "Jack Frost nipping at your nose…" from the record player in the living room, I swallowed a bite of meatloaf with ketchup glaze, one of my favorites, then said, "Mom, what did you think of Officer Lum? Good guy?"

Becky glared at me from across the table.

"Oh, come on, Nate! This is supper! It's Christmas time! Mom has had a shock; give her a break."

I found it interesting that she suddenly cared about Mom at this point in her teenage life. That was new.

Mom finished a sip of milk and held up a hand to Becky.

"It's okay, darling. I probably do need to talk about it."

She dabbed her mouth with her napkin and looked at me.

"Yes, very good guy. Very kind, dependable, and loved helping people."

I scooped my spoon under some green peas and against a slice of meatloaf.

"What cases did he have on his plate? Anything important?"

"He was working on several things, and I guess you could say they were all important. The stolen bicycle was important to the Rayburn family, and there was a pile of parking and speeding tickets accumulated by the Aldersons that had to be dealt with. But a couple of things had come in from Raleigh in the last couple of weeks that really had him busy. They had him worried, as I recall, even worried enough to discuss them with me."

I finished the peas and swallowed. It was rude to talk with food in your mouth; that was another Mammy rule.

Then I said, "If that case was from Raleigh, it must concern a statewide situation, right?"

"Well, yes and no. The car-stripping case is pretty broad, but the bootlegging case—seems we always have one of those going one—is more county wide with state implications."

She scooped a bite of mashed potatoes and gravy but held it over her plate.

"Those two were Dan's cases, but Gunner was doing some leg work for Dan on both. And that's taken away from routine patrols. We really need to hire another officer."

She ate the potatoes, swallowed, then shook her head.

"That chief of ours…You know, he's had a list of applicants, but for some reason, he's been dragging his feet."

She sighed. "But yeah, Gunner was busy. That car-stripping case was taking up so much of his time he even broke up with his girlfriend in Charlotte, the one he'd met while visiting his parents about six months ago. He'd been seeing her almost every weekend, but she wanted more."

I took a sip of milk. "How did she take it? In the movies, girlfriends don't take rejection very well."

"She wasn't happy about it, that's for sure. Fired off some hate mail at him and called him a few times at two in the morning. But she's young, nineteen, I think he said, so she's still immature."

I took the napkin out of my lap and wiped some gravy from my mouth.

"Was he okay with the breakup?"

"Oh yeah. He'd been considering that for, oh…several weeks. No, he wasn't upset at all; I'd say more relieved than upset. Besides, he'd been seeing a girl in Fayetteville who lives a lot closer and was less demanding. She's young too—nineteen, maybe twenty—but apparently more mature than Elsa." She looked up. "Elsa is the Charlotte girl."

Becky leaned in. "Two girlfriends at the same time? Sounds like a cad to me."

"Well, he was handsome—short, but handsome—kind, fit, intelligent, steady job…all the things girls look for."

Becky scoffed. "Except faithful."

"Now, Becky. He never promised either of those girls any-thing."

"Ha. That's his story."

Granddaddy, sitting very quietly at the head of the table, turned his head away, coughed into his napkin, cleared his throat, and looked at Mom and me.

"If this chapter of *Search for Tomorrow* is finished, please pass the rolls and jam." He grinned. "Quite entertaining, though. I never realized Lum was such a lady's man."

I handed him the plate with the last two rolls on it. He took it, placed it in front of his plate, and then picked up a roll. That was another etiquette thing from Mammy; you don't take something off the plate while someone is holding it for you as a servant would. You take the plate, then serve yourself.

With a sly smile and a nod to Granddaddy, Mom passed the jam to me, and I passed it on.

Becky stabbed a pea with her fork.

"Huh. I still say he was a cad."

After I helped clear the table, I washed the dishes; it was my turn again.

Meanwhile, Mom and Becky got the Christmas decorations from the hall closet.

Granddaddy and I had already mounted the tree in our tree stand and had set it up in front of the far window in the living room. The metal stand had a red bowl for water and green legs that curved up through the bowl's edges and up the tree's trunk. The legs attached to the tree with screws through the top of each of the three legs. Dad had bought that tree stand the Christmas before he left with his squadron for Korea. I could never set it up without thinking of the one time we got to set it up together and how the tree that year seemed to have a mind of its own. It took half a roll of duct tape before Dad finally got it to stand at attention.

When I finished in the kitchen, I walked through the dining room, turned right into the living room, then stopped at the light show. Two strings of bright lights, including the string of bubble lights, lay stretched across the living room carpet. As happened every Christmas, a couple of strings next to the others, but plugged into the same extension cord, lay cold and dark.

Mom looked up from her kneeling position on the floor.

"Just in time, Nate. Open the end-table drawer and get out the extra bulbs, please." She smiled. "The search for the burned-out bulbs is on."

It took eight new light bulbs to get all the strings lit, and all the new bulbs were green because green was the only color Pace's Department Store had. Mom remembered to stock up that year too late to get the pack with the mixed colors.

Meanwhile, Becky, working beside me on the opposite end of the string from Mom, whispered, "There's another girl Lum the cad was dating."

She glanced around to make sure Mom wasn't looking and Granddaddy was still in the kitchen. "Gill's sister, Rachel—a senior at good ol' Southern Pines High School."

"You're kidding."

"Nope. Seventeen. Bet we see her at the funeral."

"Wow."

As Dean Martin sang "Sleigh Bells" from the record player, I looked over at Mom.

"Hey, Mom. How old was Officer Lum?"

She looked up and gazed across the room.

"Oh, well, his birthday was coming up soon, January something. I think he was going to be…twenty-six."

Becky and I turned to each other with mouths open. *The man was robbin' the cradle!*

We returned to replacing bulbs, then I whispered, "Lum and Rachel. How long?"

"Just recently. Maybe two dates—dinner in Aberdeen, a walk in Pinehurst."

"And what did Gill think about that?"

"Hey, what are you two whispering about over there?"

Mom had stood and held the end of the string of bubble lights. They always went on first because they were the heaviest and needed the strongest limbs.

Becky looked up. "Oh, we were talking about Gill."

"Yeah, I liked Gill. Very polite young man."

She turned her back to us and stepped to the tree, which stood in front of the window closest to the side wall. Meanwhile, Granddaddy's fire in the fireplace had burned down to a nice crackle and glow. Mom raised the first bubble light to the top section of the tree.

"Join up, kids. Need some wingmen over here to help string these lights."

Mom liked to use Dad's old Marine pilot expressions and lingo.

As we stood, Granddaddy, who had apparently returned from the kitchen with a fresh cup of coffee and had sat quietly on the sofa behind us, leaned over to us.

"Well, what *did* Gill think of that?"

We always seemed to underestimate the old veteran's hearing as well as Mom's.

Thirty minutes later, the finished tree glistened with bright colored lights, including a lot of green ones. Shiny, glittering balls of all shapes, sizes, and colors, plus a string of gold garland and strips of silver tinsel, hung from the limbs. At the bottom, we always had a white sheet wrapped and piled around the tree stand to represent snow. That was Mom's task. The finishing touch was the silver star on the top point of the tree, which had been Dad's job, but since his death, it had been Becky's— the firstborn. That year, 1955, she did it without falling off the step ladder and onto the tree, which happened her first year on the job—1952. You know I enjoyed that.

With Sunday papers to deliver in the morning, I went to bed early. Wearing last year's blue pajamas and with my hands locked behind my head, I lay in my twin bed in the dark in the bedroom I shared with Granddaddy. I thought of Lum's cases—the Rayburns, the Aldersons, car stripping, bootlegging. I had to believe one of those cases was connected to his murder. I'd start with the Rayburns. They were on my paper route, and their son, Jimmy, was in my class at school and my Sunday school class at church. I doubted anyone would kill to keep from being nabbed for bicycle theft, but in rural North Carolina, anything was possible. Then, as Mammy had taught me years before, I took some long, deep breaths and fell asleep.

The next morning, Tom Ray, the village bully and career sixth grader with the ice-blue eyes, joined me to run my paper route. Over the last few months, we'd become friends and done well. Plus, in school, I had helped him with history, he had helped me with math, and after that half year ended, he would be promoted to the seventh grade. That still had him a grade behind, but he was on his way up, doing good. With the news of his promotion, the Fryfogel twins and the other kids in my sixth-grade class, afraid the old Tom Ray would reappear at any time, had sighed a huge sigh of relief. "Big Fry," the big twin in the horn-rimmed glasses, even bought me a round of chocolate milk in the lunch room when word got around that Tom Ray was moving up. So, I was surprised when Tom Ray showed up at 4:30 a.m. that frosty Sunday morning to wrap papers with me and said he had to quit.

In the pale light from our front stoop and the streetlight across the street, I looked up from my kneeling position in our gravel driveway and pushed my blue baseball cap further off my forehead.

"What?" Even though I wore a wool coat and scarf, that news sent a chill through me. I mean, it shocked me. That was the last thing I expected him to say.

Kneeling across from me in a black watch cap and threadbare brown coat, he finished fastening a rubber band to another paper and hung his head.

"Yeah, sorry, Nate, but some things have come up, and I won't be able to do this anymore."

"Like what? What's come up? We're doing good here, and we're making money. You got your bike. I got my glove. I don't get it."

Still looking at the pile of papers, he shook his head.

"Yeah, I know, but it's not my decision. I'd like to keep working the route with you, but I can't. This will have to be my last day." He looked up. "And you don't have to pay me for today."

I collapsed back onto my heels.

"Well, geez, Tom Ray. I hate this." I leaned back over the pile of papers and slid an insert into the top one. "And of course I'll pay you for today."

I wrapped and banded the paper, then leaned back on my heels again.

"Hey, maybe you could do it again later, say in a few weeks?"

He shook his head.

"Ah, I don't think so. We're moving."

"Moving? When? Can't you at least finish this week? You could use a little more Christmas money, right?"

"I wish I could, but I can't. We leave after school is out Wednesday."

Well, that's how that Sunday morning started. I couldn't get any more out of him, but after he pedaled off to cover his customers and I'd pedaled off with my basket and chest pack full of papers to cover mine, I remembered I'd seen a strange car at his house the last few days—a black pickup truck. I also remembered that even in the pale light from our stoop, the left side of his head looked bruised, and his left eye was red.

At 6:35 a.m., after an uneventful route and without an opportunity to talk with Jimmy Rayburn, I got home with Jack-Frost hands and nose and fell into bed for my usual post-route Sunday nap. I was awakened by a gentle rocking motion on my shoulder and the smell of bacon in the air. I opened my eyes.

Granddaddy, our Sunday morning chef, smiled at me.

"Reveille, Nate. Fall out for chow."

I nodded, muttered a sleepy, "Yes, sir," and threw off my

covers. My Mickey Mouse alarm clock, which I'd outgrown years ago, showed 8:28.

A few minutes later, I walked into the kitchen in my favorite long-sleeved quarter-zip shirt, jeans, and tennis shoes—the ones with a couple of drops of tobacco juice on them.

Granddaddy stood in front of the stove in his plaid bedroom slippers from last Christmas. His old World War I army sweater hung from his shoulders and over his baggy jeans. He turned a strip of bacon and nodded toward the refrigerator.

"How 'bout pouring the orange juice for us, Nate?"

"Sure." I looked at our red Formica and steel kitchen table by the wall. "And set the table?"

"Oh yeah. I thought Becky would be in here by now to do that. I woke her and your mother right after you."

He cocked his head. "But I think I hear the shower running, so they'll be here shortly."

I got the cotton placemats, silverware, and napkins from the counter drawer on the other side of the kitchen. I set the places the way Mammy had taught me and looked up.

"Granddaddy, your friend, Mr. Fat Pat…Is he still friends with Tom Ray's mother, Mrs. Urdenbach?"

"Oh yeah. Still carrying the torch but still just good friends."

He looked over at me with raised eyebrows and a half grin.

"Why do you ask, my curious one?"

I walked over and leaned against the refrigerator.

"Tom Ray quit this morning."

"Huh? I thought you boys were doing good. Did he say why?"

"They're moving this week."

He put a strip of bacon on the plate he had covered with a paper napkin.

"And you want me to ask Fat Pat if he knows anything about it."

"Yes, sir. If he hasn't told you anything about it already."

"All he's told me is that her husband is back in town. That was Friday when he relieved me at the maintenance shop for the weekend."

He turned his head and coughed, then cleared his throat.

"Want me to call him? I'm sure he's at the hospital now with his feet on my desk, reading a comic book and waiting for a gurney to need wheels or something."

"After breakfast, yes, sir."

"Can do. Meanwhile, don't forget the orange juice."

I grinned. "Yes, sir. Orange juice and milk coming up."

After breakfast, which included our traditional Sunday cinnamon rolls, my favorite breakfast food, I let Superman run around in the backyard for a few minutes. Then we got dressed and went to Sunday school, which meant I had to wear a coat and tie.

After Sunday school class and on the right side of the hallway leading to the church nave, I met up with Jimmy Rayburn at the water fountain.

As I started with, "Hey, Jimmy, I've got a question for you," a few girls, including Mary Elizabeth Chippenvale, who Charlie and I called "Chipper," walked past us in their frilly Sunday dresses. They disappeared into the girl's restroom.

Jimmy's eyes followed them. "Did, did you just smell Palmolive soap?"

"Yeah, I did."

"Yeah, yeah, girls are always so clean."

He leaned over the fountain to take a drink.

I tugged on the sleeve of his brown sport coat.

"Hey, what's this about your bike being stolen?"

He straightened, wiped his mouth on his sleeve, then gave his head a quick rub through his short, blond buzz cut.

"Yeah, yeah, last week, Thursday. I came out to mount up and go to school, and it was missing from my porch."

"Was it new? I don't remember it at school."

"Yeah, yeah, a brand-new beautiful red Schwinn with a headlight and everything. My grandparents gave it to me for Christmas. They were here visiting from High Point for a few days and brought it with them."

He checked the hallway.

"Dad is ticked. I should have put it in the garage."

"Any leads on who took it?"

"Officer Lum—hey, sorry to hear about him, Nate. I know your mother knew him and worked with him."

"Yeah, she really liked him. Good guy. But what about him and your bike?"

"Oh, oh, well, Officer Lum came by the house that afternoon and took some notes. He also fussed at me about leaving it on the porch."

"Did he say anything about finding it?"

"He said he'd do his best, but there was a ring of bike thieves working the county, and it was probably gone for good."

He took a backward step toward the nave and glanced in that direction.

"We better go."

I joined him, and at the same time, Chipper and Donna, the tall brunette and principal's daughter, walked out of the girl's room.

Donna hustled off, but Chipper, who was a dead ringer for Annette Funicello, my favorite Mouseketeer with curly brown hair and dark eyebrows, joined us.

"Hello, boys. What were you guys talking about over by the water fountain?"

I grinned. "We were talking about how nosey girls are."

She gently pushed me into Jimmy and looked at him.

"Nate lies a lot, Jimmy, so I'll ask you: What was the chat about back there?"

"My missing bike."

"Oh yeah, I heard about that. Well, any progress on the case?"

We stopped at the entrance to the nave, and Jimmy saw his parents waving to him from their pew near the front.

"Got, got to go, but Officer Lum said whoever stole it would probably sell it somewhere else in the state. That was happening a lot around Moore County."

He waved to his parents and took a step, but I grabbed his coat.

"Did he have any leads?"

"Yeah, yeah, but I've gotta go."

He jerked the coat out of my grasp and quick-walked down toward his parents and little sister, who was also a blonde.

Chipper pulled me aside to let others pass.

"Okay, Nate, tell me you haven't opened another case without telling me about it."

I waved to Mom and Becky in the third row of pews from the back. Mom pumped her fist up and down in the military "hurry up" motion.

"Got to go, Mary Elizabeth, but you know everything I know about the bike."

I took a step, but she grabbed my arm.

"Whoa. I'm not talking about the stolen bike."

"No? What else?"

"What else? Officer Lum's death, that's what else—the corpse in the Christmas tree, remember?"

She winked. "I know about that, and I may have something for you."

I winked back. "Love to hear it. Parking lot after church. Back row. Bye."

After the service, I skipped the greeting line and beat feet for the parking lot. I waited by a bare dogwood tree on the corner of the back row for a minute, then Chipper, wearing a blue coat over her dress, broke out of the crowd and walked toward me. She waved. A few seconds later, she stopped in front of me.

"I saw you skip the line, Nate, so I did too."

"So, whatcha got for me?"

A middle-aged couple passed us with a nod. We smiled and nodded back.

Chipper looked around like she was checking for eavesdroppers, then leaned toward me.

"I've heard that Officer Lum might have been seen out with a high school girl, and some people weren't happy about it."

"Who people? Who wasn't happy?"

"Two of the biggest, meanest men in the county—Junior and Jasper Barnes."

"Oh boy. I've already had a run-in with Mr. Jasper, so I know what you mean. Who's the girl?"

She glanced back toward the church and saw her parents walking toward us. Her tall, dark-complexioned father waved to her and pointed toward the first row.

"Look, can you come to my house this afternoon for cocoa and cookies?"

I held out my hand.

"I'll be there, but who's the girl?"

With a smile, she backed up toward her parents.

"I'll tell you later. And bring Charlie."

She broke into a jog but looked back at me and yelled, "Three o'clock!"

Chapter 4

NOT ABOVE MURDER

After a quick lunch of tomato soup and a grilled-cheese sandwich, I stepped up to our black phone at the end of the kitchen counter. I called Charlie and told him what I'd learned about Jimmy's bike and what Mom had said to me about Lum's case with the Aldersons. I didn't mention the other, more serious cases or Lum's girlfriends and the connection one of them had to the tobacco-spitting Goliath, Jasper Barnes. I thought I'd save that for our meeting with Chipper. Then I told him Chipper wanted us to meet her at three o'clock.

"Good. My little brother's Cub Scout den is meeting here this afternoon. It's their Christmas get-together, and I want an excuse to vanish."

Then he added. "Hey, you know what? That little Alderson kid—the eight-year-old—is in that den. What say I ask him a few friendly questions before I come over? He might spill something. Oh, remember the three guys in the old black pickup at the tree farm—the landscape guys?"

"Yeah, you got something on them?"

"Maybe. I saw my neighbor in his yard inspecting their work last evening and asked him about them. You remember my neighbor, right—the retired railroad guy who looks like Elmer Fudd but hits 'em long and straight like Ben Hogan?"

"The bald guy who wears those knickers and argyle socks from the twenties?"

"That's the guy. He's a sport, isn't he?"

"Yeah, sure is, but a nice guy."

"Yes, he is, but listen…He said those guys are from Raleigh and work for a guy from here but doesn't live here."

"Okay…"

"Yeah, well, get this: The guy's name—the guy they work for—is Urdenbach."

"Urdenbach? Tom Ray's father?"

"Gotta be. How many Urdenbachs could there be in this state?"

"Yeah. Well, I guess he could be an uncle, but…."

"Well, here's the kicker: They were supposed to finish cleaning up the planting beds yesterday, but when they showed up after lunch, a newer black pickup drove up right after them. They chatted with the driver of the newer truck, then both trucks drove off, and my neighbor hasn't seen or heard from them since."

"Kinda suspicious goings-on there, Black Dog."

"I think so."

"So, you want to come down here, and then we go to Chipper's together?"

"Strength in numbers, Kemosabe. See you about quarter 'til."

"Roger, but before you go…that stuff I told you about Jimmy's bike and the Aldersons a minute ago?"

"Yeah."

"Well, Mom told us that at supper last night in a moment of melon…melon-something. What's the word, Charlie?"

"Melancholy? Sadness?"

"Yeah, melancholy. She was still thinking of what happened to Officer Lum and feeling sad about it, distracted. I don't think she would have told us about a case or cases at the SPPD otherwise, so let's keep that between us, okay?"

"Sure."

"Okay. See you later."

I hung up and looked around. Granddaddy was still in his workshop, Mom was in the living room with her *Good Housekeeping* magazines, and Becky was in the room she shared with Mom listening to the radio. It sounded like the Drifters version of "White Christmas" was playing. I imagined her primping and admiring herself in front of the full-length mirror. She did that a lot.

After I'd put my windbreaker on over my long-sleeved, quarter-zip shirt, I stepped out the backdoor to see about Superman. Then I planned to talk with Granddaddy about daddy Urdenbach. As soon as I opened the backdoor, I smelled burning leaves, probably from the big yard and colonial house on the other side of the wire fence behind us.

As I closed the door, Superman eased out of his house, stretched out his front paws, and pressed his chest down into a big stretch with an accompanying loud yawn. He raised, shook, then looked at me with bright eyes like, *If I sit for you, will I get a treat?*

The day still hadn't come when he would sit for me just to please me.

I opened his gate. He trotted out and went straight for the first tall, long-leaf pine in our backyard. Later, I threw his old tennis ball for him a couple of times. As usual, he wouldn't bring it back the second time, so I let him ignore it. He trotted back into his house, and I shut the gate.

I walked to the garage door in front of our car and knocked our secret knock—two knocks, then three knocks. The big door that swung open to the left was fixed in place, but in a couple of seconds, the right door creaked open, and Granddaddy waved me in.

Under the two bright fluorescent light fixtures in the ceiling and amid the smell of turpentine and wood stain, I stopped next to his long workbench. Beside me stood the tall shelves he was finishing for Mom and Becky—a Christmas present only he and I knew about.

He coughed and then wiped his hands on a rag.

"What's up, Nate?"

"Granddaddy, did you get a chance to call Mr. Fat Pat?"

"Oh yeah, I did. Not much to tell though."

He tossed the rag onto the bench, then backed against it, turned his head, and coughed again.

"Ray Urdenbach is back in Libby's life all right, but Fat Pat hadn't talked with her since Friday. She didn't say anything Friday about them moving, so he was surprised to hear that."

"Has she said anything to him about what Mr. Urdenbach is doing and where he's living?"

"Raleigh, as I recall, and he's landscaping." He smiled. "Is that important?"

"Yes, sir. Could be."

He crossed his arms over his old army sweater and smiled again.

"Now, Nate, you know your mother doesn't want you playing detective, so if that's what you're up to, I don't want to know about it."

I smiled back. "Yes, sir. If that's what I'm up to, I won't tell you. But thanks for the information, and if you get a chance to learn more about Mr. Urdenbach, will you tell me?"

He chuckled. "In a casual, family-conversation way, you bet."

I left the garage in time to see Charlie wheel his bike into the backyard and slide to a stop. I checked my Timex; It was 2:35 p.m.

"You're early."

"Had to get out of there."

He dismounted and popped his kickstand into place.

As I walked toward the backdoor, he stuffed his hands into the pockets of his denim jacket and joined me.

"Nate ol' buddy, remind me never to be a den mother. Those kids are running around the house like stray cats and eating everything in sight. We've already lost two balls off the Christmas tree—knocked off, then crushed by the herd. My dad stuck his head out of his office and jokingly told Mom, 'Tell them to go outside and play in the street.'"

Charlie frowned. "I think he was joking."

"Did you learn anything from young Master Alderson?"

He snickered. "Yeah. I learned he was hungry and had to go to the bathroom."

"Nothing about speeding tickets or Officer Lum?"

"When I asked if he'd ever met a policeman, he said, 'Daddy doesn't like policemen.'"

"That's it?"

"That's it. Mom was running them outside for a relay race or something, so he had to find his jacket—which turned up behind Mom's potted corn plant in the foyer."

He rubbed his chin. "I tell you, Nate. That is one scruffy-looking kid—matted hair, dirty fingernails, dirty shoes. Mom had to scrub him down in the bathroom sink before snack time."

"Hmm. I guess if Daddy doesn't like policemen, that's something." I opened the backdoor. "Let me tell Mom I'm leaving, and then I want to make a pass by the Urdenbach's before we head over to Chipper's."

Tom Ray Urdenbach lived down our quiet little street toward town and a block to the left on Ridge Street. We had to walk by his house every weekday morning on our way to school, and in the past, that had been a trial by fire; he was deadly with a slingshot and would sometimes take shots at us and others as we passed. But those days were behind us, so that afternoon, I didn't hesitate to ride by his house and check his driveway. Empty. Even his mom's old '38 Plymouth coupe was gone.

Just past his house, we turned right, down a block, then

right again onto May Street. A few blocks later, we stopped in the front yard of the Chippenvales' and dismounted.

We jogged up the brick steps, crossed their wide porch, then stepped up to their large white door. I knocked on the brass knocker. Then Charlie leaned over, and he knocked it again.

I looked at him like, *What was that for?*

He grinned.

From inside, I thought I heard Chipper say, "They're here!"

Chipper, in her saddle oxfords and a pink dress, opened the door, greeted us with that brown-eyed Chipper smile that lights up a room, then led us a few steps down the hall. She turned right, walked between two doors that slid into the walls on either side, then led us into the living room, or maybe it was a parlor. I noticed the smell of cookies, burning logs from the fireplace against the far wall of the room, and the scent of pine from the lavishly decorated eight-foot Christmas tree. The tree stood in front of the picture window overlooking the front porch.

Chipper went straight to the electric wall plug under the window and plugged in the cord that lit the lights on the tree. She turned and smiled.

"We don't burn the lights during the day—dries out the tree."

I nodded. "So, we get lights *and* cookies?" I looked at Charlie. "Well, I feel pretty special. How about you?"

"Indubitably."

I rolled my eyes. *Show-off.*

Chipper gestured for us to sit on the pale-blue sofa in the

center of the room. It sat perpendicular to the fireplace and faced a long oak coffee table with a small stack of magazines in the center—travel magazines, as I recall. We took our seats, with me closest to the fireplace. Two stuffed wing chairs with large blue-and-gray stripes faced us from the other side of the coffee table. Chipper sat in the one directly across from me but then hopped back up.

"I'll go help Mom, boys. Be right back."

The room had paneled walls, floor-to-ceiling built-in bookshelves on either side of the fireplace, and an oil portrait of a blonde woman in a long, white wedding dress above the mantel. The scene reminded me of one of those old detective movies where a rich gray-haired guy in a smoking jacket stands before a fireplace in a room full of heavy furniture. He lights his pipe and then asks Phillip Marlowe, or Sam Spade, or maybe Michael Shayne to find his missing daughter *and* keep his name out of the papers. The focal point in that room was the oil portrait—Chipper's beautiful blond mother with the peekaboo hairstyle.

A minute later, I heard the *click-click-click* of a dog's nails on the hardwood. Sofie, their spaniel, followed by Chipper, then her mom in a long red dress and pearls, walked through the wide entrance.

Charlie and I stood. I mean, that's what gentlemen do when a lady enters the room.

Chipper carried a tray with three mugs full of hot chocolate topped with tiny marshmallows. Her mother carried a tray of sugar cookies cut into Christmas shapes and topped with colored icing. They placed the trays on the coffee table.

Sofie nuzzled my leg, so I bent over and gave her a scratch behind her ears.

Her mother said, "Please take your seats, boys. Be comfortable."

We sat, and Chipper sat opposite me again.

Her mother walked around and behind the sofa. She stopped between us, placed a hand on each of us, and said, "Good to see you again, boys."

Then she leaned over and whispered, "But I've been told not to hang around, so I'll be leaving now." She winked. "Come back soon."

She looked at Sofie. "Come on, Sofie."

We leaned forward to stand.

"No, no, keep your seats." She walked out, and Sofie followed.

Chipper handed out napkins.

"Okay, Nate, where were we?"

I plopped a couple of cookies onto my napkin.

"You said you had something to tell me about the Barnes family of Goliaths. They weren't happy about a high school girl seeing Officer Lum or something like that."

"Yeah, more than unhappy. They wanted to do something about it."

"Who was the girl? And what did they plan to do?"

"Her name is Rachel, a senior at our high school, and I was told they planned to 'forcefully discourage' Officer Lum."

I heard a sharp crunch from Charlie and looked over to see him with half a cookie in his hand and a white marshmallow mustache on his upper lip. He stopped chewing and shrugged.

Of course, I'd already heard the girl's name from Becky, but the Barneses' plan to handle the situation was new.

"Who told you this?" I took a careful sip of my hot chocolate.

"Her little sister, Patty. She's in my Sunday school class. You may have seen her in school; she's twelve and already taller than all the boys in her class. They grow 'em big in that Turner family."

Charlie pointed his second cookie at Chipper.

"'Forcefully discouraging' and 'killing' are pretty far apart."

Chipper shrugged. "It is, so they may not be our perps, but that's what Patty said."

I nodded. "Okay, so the Barnes family has a motive—not much of a motive, but they have a motive."

Charlie toasted me with his mug of hot chocolate.

"And they knew that field would be burned. Don't forget that."

"Yeah, good point." I looked at Chipper. "That field of Fraser firs where I found the body was scheduled to be burned today."

She brightened. "And the body and the evidence destroyed. Hey, the plot thickens."

"Yep, and to add to the girlfriend angle, Lum was also dating a nineteen-year-old in Charlotte—Elsa something—who he had just broken up with, and another nineteen-year-old in Fayetteville."

"Humph. He liked 'em young."

Charlie reached for another cookie.

"And as we've learned from many a Saturday crime movie,

my friends, it's the younger woman who leads a good man to ruin."

Chipper and I shared a smile, and then she looked at Charlie.

"And, as I recall, the jilted younger woman isn't just satisfied with ruin—she's not above murder. If you ask me, that Elsa girl is as good a suspect as the Barnes men."

We nodded, then I elbowed Charlie.

"Look, let's go see Detective Lewis after school tomorrow. We still have that standing invitation to tell him about your family history. Maybe he'll let us in on what he's learned—like how Officer Lum died and when."

"That's a thin 'maybe,' but I'm with you. Tomorrow it is. And hey, maybe he'll also tell us who, besides the Barnes brothers and Gill, knew that field would be burned. That is if he knows."

"Another thin maybe and a very thin 'if,' but it can't hurt to ask."

As we pedaled home to the *squeak-squeak* of my front tire hitting the edge of my front fender, which I'd been meaning to fix, I glanced at Charlie.

"I didn't mention this to Chipper, but Officer Lum had a couple of other cases on his plate—cases that may be more important than the dating thing, the Alderson ticket thing, or the stolen bike thing."

Charlie swung his head and long hair side to side with each stroke of the pedals.

"Yeah?"

"Yeah, but remember, what I tell you is confidential. We're not supposed to know this."

He looked at me and grinned. "It's okay. I got it."

"Okay. Now, I've been thinking about what you told me earlier—the landscaping guys and Urdenbach. I found the body yesterday; the landscaping guys, who work for Urdenbach, suddenly left the job they were on yesterday, then Tom Ray suddenly quit today. Plus, as of last Friday, Mrs. Urdenbach apparently didn't know they were moving."

"Whoa, wait a minute. Tom Ray quit? You didn't tell me that."

"This morning. Said they were moving Wednesday after school. Didn't say where."

"Wow. Then that Urdenbach probably was his father." He shook his head. "Sounds like the gang knows the marshal's onto 'em, and they're pullin' out of Dodge."

We passed the turn up to my house on Orchard Road.

"Hey, where are you going?"

"One more pass by the Urdenbachs. That okay?"

"Sure. If he's moving, he's probably already packed his slingshot."

We continued on May, then looped back up to Ridge Street. We rode past the Urdenbachs' on Ridge—still quiet, almost like they were already gone—then turned up Orchard Road.

I stopped when we got to Mr. Barrow's long, curved, tree-lined driveway on our right.

Charlie stopped beside me.

Mr. Barrow owned the five acres of Barrow's Wood across

the street from our house and lived in a large, two-story, stone Victorian house with turrets and a widow's walk. We couldn't see that house from where we were, but we could see the front of the old two-story carriage house. It stuck out of the woods on the left side of the sand and clay driveway about a hundred yards down.

I turned to Charlie. "You got time for a visit with Mr. Barrow?"

He glanced up at the sky. A layer of dark gray clouds had left us in dim twilight.

"Okay, but make it a quick one. I told Mom I'd be back before dark."

I pushed off and turned down the driveway. "A quick one it is."

Charlie pedaled up beside me. "You gonna tell me about those other cases or not? You left off at the Urdenbachs' move."

"Oh, yeah, the cases. Well, they deal with a car-stripping ring and a bootlegging ring."

"Man, either Urdenbach or Barnes could be into that stuff."

"Agree. I want to see if Mr. Barrow knows anything. That man knows everyone in Moore County."

I glanced at Charlie. "And what they're up to."

Chapter 5

THE HEARTBREAKER

A t Mr. Barrow's stone steps, we kicked our kickstands into place, then stepped up to the massive, wooden front door. I pulled the handle beside the door and heard the *clang, clang* echo inside.

Charlie pushed his hair back over his ears and whispered, "This place still gives me the creeps."

A few seconds later, the door creaked open. The butler, Wickers, in his penguin outfit, stepped into the doorway. His bent nose and tall, thick frame gave away his former wrestling career and blotted out the light from inside.

Stone-faced as usual, he said in his bored monotone, "Ah, Master Nathan." He looked at Charlie. "And Master Charlie, the werewolf as I recall from Halloween."

Charlie smiled. "That was me, and thank you again for that Hershey bar."

"You're welcome. Are you boys back for another Hershey bar?"

I chuckled. "No, Mr. Wickers. Of course, we wouldn't turn

one down, but I'm here to speak with Mr. Barrow." I nodded. "If I may."

"Certainly. Come in, and I'll announce you. Mr. Barrow is reading the paper."

Wickers led us through the marble foyer, past the medieval knight dressed in chainmail with sword and shield who stood against the wall, then onto the polished hardwood floor of the sitting area. Mr. Barrow, cigar in hand and dressed in a maroon robe and matching slippers, sat in his leather rocker facing the fireplace, a fireplace big enough to roast a boar hog. He looked up and over his horn-rimmed readers.

Wickers nodded toward us. "Master Nate and Master Charlie, sir."

Mr. Barrow smiled his weak smile. "Hello, boys."

He folded the paper and set it on the ornate table with the Tiffany lamp to his right.

"You may go, Wickers."

"Very good, sir."

Wickers, as quiet as he was large, drifted out of the room to the right.

Mr. Barrow, who looked like Boris Karloff with a gray mustache, placed his hands on his thin thighs.

"Nate. Good to see you. And your friend, ah…"

"Charlie, Mr. Barrow. The werewolf."

He nodded and pulled on his mustache.

"Ah yes, Charlie the werewolf. Good to see you again, Charlie."

"Good to see you again, Mr. Barrow. You're looking good."

"Thank you."

He puffed his cigar and pointed to the red leather chair to his right and on the other side of the table.

"Got a chair for one of you, or we can move to the back of the room. There's plenty of comfortable seating behind us."

"No, thank you, sir. We only have a minute. We were both supposed to be home before dark." I glanced at Charlie and then back to Mr. Barrow.

"I suppose you've heard about Officer Lum's murder, sir."

"Yes, I have." He took off his glasses and rubbed his forehead. "Very unsettling. And right here is our peaceful little town."

"He was a good friend to my mother. We want to help find his killer."

He looked up. "Yes, I'm sure you do."

He set his glasses on top of the newspaper. "How can I help?"

I noticed the paper was the Raleigh Sunday paper, not the Charlotte paper I had delivered to him that morning.

"Are you taking the Raleigh paper again, sir?"

"No, Wickers picked this up for me this morning. I'm going to Raleigh tomorrow for a meeting of the NCADA, the car dealers association. I'm a past chairman and on the executive committee. I just wanted to catch up on what was going on over there. State capital, you know."

He smiled. "Don't want to be left out of any conversations."

"Oh, Raleigh. That's great. Was there anything in there about a car-stripping ring?"

He picked up the paper.

"I believe there was. It seems I read something about that. Want me to look?"

"If you don't mind, sir. One of the things Officer Lum was working on was a statewide car-stripping ring out of Raleigh."

He put his glasses back on, popped the paper open, then turned to the second page.

"I'm sure it wasn't on the first page. Murders, accidents, and bad weather are on the front, you know. Disasters sell papers."

He scanned the second page, then looked over at the third page.

"Ah, here it is, the bottom of page three." He looked up.

"What would you like to know?"

"Any progress on the case?"

"Ah, 'following up on leads…all law enforcement offices in the state on alert…no one in custody.'" He looked up again. "None. No progress." He folded the paper.

"But if it deals with cars, I'll hear about it tomorrow and Tuesday. I'll be back Tuesday."

"Do you know anyone in this area who could be involved in such a thing? Maybe they have a history of something like this."

"Stock car racing is big in this state and certainly in this area as well, so there are a lot of people around here who know how to take cars apart and put them back together. I don't know anyone who has been involved with stealing and stripping cars, but if I had to suspect someone of doing such a thing, it would be Buster Barnes. Another would be Ray Urdenbach. Ray raced for Buster when he was still a teenager."

Bingo. "Is Buster Barnes related to Junior and Jasper Barnes?"

"Their father."

"And the bootlegging. Anyone come to mind?"

He scoffed. "Where to begin? They're everywhere."

"No one in particular?"

"The last one to get caught at it was Looper Heister over on the Carthage Road. He did some time, as I recall, but he's been out a year or so now. His boys might have taken up the trade in his absence and still be running some, or Looper could be back at it."

He pointed his paper at me.

"But leave those people alone, Nate—both families, the Barneses and the Heisters. They are mean, mean people, especially the Barnes boys—Junior and Jasper. Back when I was mayor, they were suspected of killing a high school classmate. Never proven, but the boy, I think his name was Kenner, reportedly made some disparaging remarks about their mother, disappeared soon after, and has not been heard from since. We suspected the body was buried on their farm, but we never found it."

He pointed at me again. "Don't mess with them."

A few minutes later, and with Mr. Barrow's compliments, we pedaled away from his house with a large Hershey bar each from the stock Wickers kept for Mr. Barrow. That man had a serious sweet tooth…like Charlie, who waved goodbye to me when I turned into our driveway.

Our car sat in front of the garage. Light streamed from the side window of the garage, meaning Granddaddy was back at work on the shelves. I stashed my bike against Superman's fence and opened the gate for him.

He crawled out of his house, stretched, then looked at me like, *Well?*

"Yes, I know. You're hungry, right?"

He stood tall and gave me that goofy grin of his like, *You got it, boss, now bring on the grits.*

After I told Mom I was home, I fed the beast his canned Friskies dog food, not grits. While he gulped it down, I freshened his water.

When I got back inside, Mom was at the stove stirring a steaming pot of green beans. I heard the sound of silverware and plates in the dining room, so I assumed that was Becky setting the table. I hugged Mom, then whispered, "Ever heard of Buster Barnes or Looper Heister?"

She stirred the beans. "Oh yeah. Looper's the one who shot Chief McDonald."

"Shot him? You mean like with a thirty-eight?"

"I mean like with a shotgun."

"Oh. Hey, the limp! Is that how he got the limp? I thought it was from World War Two."

She scoffed.

"In World War Two, he was 'in the rear with the gear,' as your father would say. He was a clerk typist at some army headquarters. But yeah, he got the limp after he found Looper's still and tried to arrest him. Looper saw him coming and shot him."

She reached for the slotted spoon in the spoon cradle. "He did time for it."

"Wow. Any run-ins with Mr. Heister lately?"

She spooned beans into a serving bowl.

"Not that I know of. His boys have been in trouble a few times—assault, speeding, routine Heister family stuff."

"But no more bootlegging?"

"Don't think so, but Dan might know. He's got their file."

I briefly heard a blast of Little Richard music from Mom and Becky's room. I figured Becky had gone back into the room, turned on the radio, then shut the door, so I could speak up.

"Mom, how about the Barnes family? What are they into?"

She smiled. "You mean other than Christmas trees?"

"Yes, ma'am."

"I think I've said enough already, Nate. Besides, it's time to eat."

She nodded toward the backdoor.

"If you'll go get Granddaddy, I'll put everything on the table."

"Yes, ma'am, but can we talk again later? I mean about the Barneses. I can help, Mom. Really. I know stuff Detective Lewis couldn't know."

She smiled and patted down my cowlick, a habit I had grudgingly accepted.

"Okay, we'll talk later. But for now..." She turned me around and swatted me on the rump. "Go get Granddaddy."

After supper, Mom decided she'd rather watch *The Jack Benny Show*, so we didn't get to talk about the Barnes family, but I did get her blessing for a visit to the SPPD the next day. I figured the coroner's report would be there by the time school was out, and we could learn how Officer Lum had died. That is if Detective Lewis would tell us. I believe he would tell us because, by that time, I would have information to trade. That's where Jimmy Rayburn would come in.

The talk before the school bell rang that crisp and clear Monday morning was all about the murder, the bike thefts, and the math test announced on the blackboard for Wednesday. We couldn't believe Mrs. Mac would give us a test on our last day before Christmas break and the same day as our Christmas party. When she confirmed it, our howls of protest didn't seem to faze her. Our frizzy-haired teacher in the polka-dot, cat-eye glasses just sat behind her big oak desk and smiled.

I shot a look across the room to Tom Ray and pleaded with my eyes, *Can you save me?*

He grimaced and shrugged.

Later, on the playground at recess, Tom Ray avoided me, but I got a chance to corner Jimmy Rayburn. I found him under the monkey bars where he'd fallen victim to Billy Westley, the guy with freckles and a gap in the teeth like Howdy Doody. They had met in the middle, and then Billy had gotten his legs around Jimmy first so that Jimmy couldn't hang on and fell. I can't remember if we had a name for that game, but Billy was quick and had strong arms, so until Tom Ray showed up, he ruled the bars.

While another hardy sixth grader waited to swing across the bars to challenge Billy, I gave Jimmy a hand up.

"Hey, Jimmy, you got time to talk about Officer Lum?"

He brushed the dirt from his jeans. "Yeah, yeah, I guess so."

I steered him toward some open ground so no one could overhear us.

"You said Lum had other leads on the bicycle thieves. Did he mention what those leads were?"

"All, all he said was that it was a large organization with representatives in almost every town." He rubbed his buzz cut.

"Oh, oh, and the local representative would get a kick-back, or commission, on every bike they located for the main people. Then they would come in at night and steal the bike."

"The local guy would give the main guys a name and address?"

"No, no, just the address and type of bike—girl or boy bike, red or blue. That kind of stuff."

"Geez. Well, I guess we could start with who knew you had a new bike."

"Yeah, yeah, except that would include almost everyone in our combined junior high and high school."

"So, you rode it to school and parked it in the bike rack by the gym."

"Yeah, yeah. Two days in a row. Then they stole it."

"And you padlocked it."

"Yeah, yeah, but remember they stole it off my porch." He hung his head.

"I should have padlocked it to a porch post or put it in the garage like Dad told me to."

"Yeah…well, you didn't, so as my mom would say, 'No point crying over spilled milk.'"

I put a hand on his shoulder.

"Hey, maybe Santa will bring you another one."

He scoffed. "Yeah, yeah, when pigs fly. I think I'm on his naughty list for good now."

"Oh, at church you mentioned leads, but Officer Lum didn't have any leads?"

He rubbed his buzz cut again. "No names, but he said he'd checked my neighborhood, and he didn't think there were any suspects there, so it might be someone from school or someone who saw me riding to school."

"But no names."

"No, no, but when I told him about Buddy Alderson making a big fuss over the bike, he kinda perked up and wrote that down. I pass their house every morning."

He looked up. "You know Buddy?"

"Ah, no I don't."

"Fifth grader."

I grimaced. "Surely a fifth grader wouldn't be in with a bunch of thieves."

"You don't know the Aldersons. Buddy might not, but his father is another story."

The bell rang, and we both looked toward the backdoor to the hallway and classrooms. We walked toward the door, and I rubbed my neck.

"Here we go, back to our cell block."

He chuckled. "Hey, did you get Mrs. Mac something for Christmas?"

"No, not yet. Any ideas?"

"No, no idea. Well…maybe cash. I heard her husband lost

his job. They may have to sell her piano, his Corvette, and maybe even have to sell their house."

"When did that happen?"

"Right after they got back from summer vacation. Then he left to go look for work in Raleigh." He shrugged. "At least that's what I heard my mom say to my dad."

And that's when it occurred to me the thieves' contact could be a teacher—or a teacher's husband.

"Okay, Billy, but remember that's just a rumor and may not be true. For now, let's give her the benefit of the doubt."

"Yeah, yeah, benefit of the doubt."

We walked a few more steps, and other kids caught up with us while a few jogged passed. Then he brightened.

"Hey, hey, I've got it. Why don't you ask for a bike for Christmas, then I can use your old bike?"

I shook my head. "Not a chance, Jimmy. I'm finally getting that pump BB gun I've been waiting on for a year."

I held the door for him, and we followed tall Donna and blonde Rose, the class beauty queen, down the hall. Rose turned and stuck out her tongue at me, and I shot my tongue back at her. She still hadn't gotten over that raw egg I had slipped into her purse last spring.

Jimmy waited inside for me.

"You, you sure about that BB gun?"

"Not guaranteed, but I've made it pretty clear that's all I want."

I considered that a second.

"Well, that and some Boy Scout stuff—canteen, cooking

set. And a couple of model airplane kits. Maybe a train set. Couple of board games. I did mention those things."

He laughed, and his laugh only added to the din of voices and laughter in that echo chamber of a hallway, so he raised his voice.

"Good luck getting all that stuff—none of us have been that good!"

Just as we got to the door to our classroom, Charlie came up behind me and grabbed my shoulder.

"Hey, we still on for this afternoon?"

"Yeah, can you go right away?"

We slipped through the doorway together.

"Got to go home first, but will three thirty be okay?"

Over the racket from giggling girls and scrapping chairs, I said, "Three thirty. My place."

I lightly punched his arm. "Got some news, Black Dog."

Charlie grinned and punched me back. "So do I, Kemosabe. So do I."

That afternoon, as I walked home from school under a clear blue sky, Charlie waved as he passed me on his bike, then I noticed Tom Ray ahead of me. I jogged to catch up and called, but he broke into a jog. By the time I got to his house, he had just stepped inside and was closing the door behind him. I slowed to a walk. When I passed his house, I noticed his mom's old '38 Plymouth coupe was back at the end of the two-lane driveway.

I got home and was looking through the mail for my new *Boy's Life* magazine when I heard a car pull into our driveway. I looked through the window in the front door and saw a black Ford roll to a stop.

Becky's buddy, Jenny, sat in the front seat while her skinny mom, with the sunken cheeks and big hair, sat at the wheel. Becky, in a white sweater and green plaid swing skirt, stepped out from the back seat. She thanked Jenny's mom, waved goodbye, then jogged up to the house. She entered with a big smile.

That post-school smile was so unusual I had to ask, "Okay, what are you so happy about?"

She shut the door, then turned and held up her arms and books like she had just scored a touchdown.

"I've been invited to the basketball game Friday night! By Gill!"

"Heck, I knew that. He told Charlie and me at the tree farm that we were invited and to bring you."

She dropped her arms. "*You* bring me?"

"Yeah, well, Mom bring *us*. Or maybe Charlie's mom will bring us."

"Oh." Head down, she walked into the dining room and set her books on the table.

"I thought he'd finally gotten that car he was saving for, and I was going to be his first date."

I saw a great opportunity to stick it to her the way she would have done me, but my tender-hearted side overruled my revengeful side.

"Well, he wanted you there to admire his performance, so that's a good sign."

She stared at her books. "Yeah. I guess."

She walked back to the end of the living room and then into her room. The door closed. I heard the radio click on, then Fats Domino singing, "Ain't That a Shame."

The phone rang.

I walked into the kitchen and answered, "Hawke residence, Nate speaking."

"Hey, it's me."

"Yeah, Charlie, what's up?"

"Can we make it four o'clock?"

"Yeah, I guess. I'll call Mom to be sure, and I'll let you know if that won't work. What's the problem?"

"Oh, I forgot to make my bed this morning, so now I've got to make the bed, rake the backyard, and bag the leaves."

"Tough break. Well, hop to it. I'll come up and help."

"Oh, great. See you in a few."

I called Mom. We were good for four o'clock, so I pedaled up to Charlie's. We knocked out the yard work and rolled back down Orchard Road to town.

On the way, Charlie said he had cornered Tom Ray at recess and learned the move had been put off until Thursday. He didn't know why and Tom Ray hadn't explained why, but he didn't sound happy about the move; it was almost like he was beginning to like school. I didn't know whether to believe that part or not.

Also, on the way, I reminded Charlie that the main thing I wanted to learn from Detective Lewis was the cause and time of death. And, of course, if he had any leads.

Charlie said, "Got to be Jasper Barnes."

As I rolled my bike into the bike rack in front of the SPPD,

I said, "Hey, you still goin' to the basketball game with us Friday?"

He rolled his into place and walked around behind it.

"Sure, but my dad may want to go, so he might drive."

"That's fine. I just thought as your mom was driving us to the dance Thursday night, we'd drive Friday. You are still going to the dance, right? I mean, that pneumonia hasn't set in yet, has it?"

He thumped his fist to his chest and coughed.

"I don't know. Could be."

"Black Dog, if you don't show, it will break little Susie Wilkerson's heart. You wouldn't want that on your conscience, would you?"

"Hey, she's young; she'll get over it." He winked. "Besides, if I show, I'm dancing with Chipper. You can dance with Susie."

"Ha! Don't count on that Chipper dance, Mr. Black Dog, famous sixth-grade heartbreaker. Those girls stick together. If you don't dance with Susie, you won't dance with anyone."

I crossed my arms. "And they'll probably write tear-jerking songs about you too—the 'He done her wrong' kind of songs. You won't be able to show—"

"Enough." He pushed me toward the walkway to the office. "Let's get serious and go find out who else knew that field would be burned."

Chapter 6

STOLEN CAR

The lobby area of the SPPD had a Coke machine and chairs on the right side, a long counter across the middle, and Mom's big rubber plant plus a window air conditioner on the left. Heat came from an electric heater inside each room. The duty officer's desk faced us and sat empty on the other side of the counter. Mom's desk sat beside it. Light came from a fluorescent light in the center of the ceiling. The place smelled a little better without Officer Lum's cigarette smoldering in the ashtray on the duty desk, but Chief McDonald smoked, so there was some of that coming from his office in the far-right corner. Detective Lewis's office was on the other side of the counter and immediately to the right.

Mom stepped out of Detective Lewis's office wearing a white cardigan sweater over a blue dress and smiled.

"Right on time, boys." She lifted the access panel on the counter and gestured us back toward Lewis's office. "Dan has cleared his desk and is waiting for you."

From inside the office, Lewis said, "Not quite cleared yet, but come on in."

We sat in the two wooden captain's chairs in front of his desk. A cold Coke sat on a paper napkin on the edge of the desk in front of each of us. We looked at each other and smiled.

Lewis, in a white shirt and blue tie with a gold clasp, slipped a file into his top drawer. He rolled up to his desk.

"Okay, boys, what do you have for me?"

I picked up my Coke and looked at Charlie.

"You go first, Charlie. Tell him about Urdenbach and your neighbor."

Charlie told the Urdenbach story—the guys in the truck, the landscaping business, the sudden departure from the job, the Urdenbach connection, and the Urdenbach family move.

Lewis took notes on a yellow pad, then looked up. "That it?"

"Yes, sir, but Tom Ray has been very defensive about it, like something's going on."

He nodded. "Okay." He looked at me. "You're up, Nate."

I swallowed. "Yes, sir."

I set my Coke back on the napkin and then wiped the moisture from my hand onto my jeans. I cleared my throat.

"To add to Charlie's story, I've learned that Mr. Urdenbach drove race cars for Buster Barnes when Mr. Urdenbach was a teenager, so both guys know cars and how to strip them. I've got more information on the bike ring, bootleggers, and car stripping, but first, I was wondering if you'd tell us what the coroner's report said—you know, time of death, cause of death."

He glanced up at Mom, who stood in the doorway with

her arms crossed. She smiled and shook her head like they shared a secret.

He looked at me.

"Bike ring, bootleggers, and car strippers?" He shook his head. "But I thought I told you boys not to play detective."

"Yes, sir, but you said don't go looking for murderers. We haven't been looking for murderers. We've just been gathering information so you can look for murderers."

"Humph. Okay, you got me there."

He pulled a manila file from a side drawer and opened it.

"I'll give you the basics, but this information cannot leave this room. Do you understand that?"

We nodded, and Charlie said, "We know. You don't want the perps to know what you know."

"That is correct. So, agreed? No talking about this to anyone?"

We said in unison, "Agreed."

"Let me see your hands and tell me again. Agreed?"

Rats. I uncrossed my fingers, and we held up our hands. "Agreed."

"Okay. Now, I'm only telling you this because you two obviously have connections I don't have, so I'm convinced you can help."

He picked up an official-looking form and looked at me.

"Our best guess is that he was killed the night before you found him or maybe late afternoon the day before. Rigor mortis was almost complete, but the cold that night may have delayed the onset so that it could have been earlier. He had a large trauma—a bruise—on his neck, but it was death by strangulation."

I looked at Charlie. "Somebody strong."

Charlie nodded. "Yeah, or with strong hands. Like a masseuse."

"Masseuse? What's that? You showing off again?"

"A massage therapist—gives people massages."

"Okay, boys, slow down. Yes, it could be a masseuse, and as it turns out, the woman Gunner was dating in Charlotte, Elsa Creech, is a masseuse."

Charlie made a fist. "Bingo! Suspect number one."

"Well, maybe. I'll get a chance to interview her here Wednesday morning; she's coming to the funeral."

I shifted in my seat. "As long as we're on the female angle, what about the girl in Fayetteville?"

"I've also had a phone conversation with her—same deal; she'll be here for the funeral, and I'll interview her afterward."

I leaned in. "Elsa Creech in the morning, then what's-her-name in the afternoon."

"Correct. And her name is Jean Ann Tuley. She's a teacher."

I glanced at Charlie and back to Lewis.

"A teacher? At age nineteen?"

"She teaches karate and judo in women's self-defense classes." He smiled. "That's why Gunner has been so sore lately—she'd been giving him private lessons."

Whoa. Two women with strong hands. I raised my Coke to Detective Lewis.

"There is one more female in this story, you know, but I doubt if she has strong hands."

"Who's that?"

"Rachel Turner."

He nodded. "Oh yeah, the high school girl."

"Yes, sir."

"Well, I've ruled her out."

"I don't mean as a suspect."

"Oh. What then?"

"For some reason, the Barnes family did not like the fact that Officer Lum was seeing Rachel."

Lewis glanced at Mom and then back to me. "So…"

"So, they were going to 'forcefully discourage' him from seeing her."

"Who told you that?"

I glanced at Charlie, and he gave me a faint head shake with squinted eyes. I looked back at Lewis.

"It's going around school. Kids are talking about it."

"Sounds like the rumor mill at school is going full speed." He checked his watch.

I shrugged. "That's what I heard. I've also heard that the Barnes family—Misters Buster, Junior, and Jasper—are not above such a thing."

"Yeah. We know about them."

He closed the coroner's report file and rechecked his watch.

I got the hint. "Ah…yes, sir. Well, I'll know more about them tomorrow afternoon."

I stood, and Charlie stood with me.

"Can we talk more tomorrow? I still want to tell you about the bike ring and the bootleggers."

"We'll see."

Inside the main office, the phone rang. Mom left the room. Charlie and I finished off our Cokes and followed.

We found Mom at her desk with the phone to her ear.

"Yes, Miss Tuley…Oh, sorry you can't make it…Yes, I understand, and I'll tell him, but he's here, and I'm sure he'll want to talk with you…No, don't hang up, Miss Tuley…Miss Tuley…?"

Tuley. I thought back to the fingers sticking out of the blanket at the tree farm and looked at Charlie. *Dum-de-dum-dum!*

That night, Monday, along with the Wednesday math test to prepare for, we also had to write an essay on a historical subject of our choice. I chose "The Founding of Naval Aviation." If it was in writing, Mom never threw it away, so I had scads of material on the Naval Air Station Pensacola in Pensacola, Florida. Dad was stationed there as a flight instructor when I was born. Plus, there was more information on Pensacola in our encyclopedias.

I sat at my desk under the side window in the bedroom I shared with Granddaddy and knocked it out in half an hour. Then I opened my math book. A second later, like a *stay of execution* from the governor, there was a knock on the door.

"Come in."

Mom opened the door wide enough to stick her head inside.

"Nate, if you've finished that essay, can you take a break and talk for a minute?"

I turned around in my folding chair and hung my arm over the back.

"Sure, Mom. Come on in. I was hoping to get a chance to talk with you tonight."

Dressed in a green Christmas sweater, she stepped into the room and closed the door.

"I bet I know why."

I grinned. "I bet you do."

I stepped over and sat on the corner of my bed.

"And I bet you want to know what else I know about Officer Lum's murder."

She sat on the corner of Grandaddy's bed with her hands on the knees of her jeans.

"Yes, my psychic son, I do." She glanced at the floor and rubbed her knees.

"That coroner's report really bothered me, Nate—a blow to the neck, then strangled. Who would do that to a nice guy just doing his job?"

I reached over and patted her hand.

"Probably someone mean enough, angry enough, or scared enough to be desperate enough to resort to murder. At least, that's usually the motive in the movies."

"Who comes to mind for you?"

"The Barnes family is mean enough; his former girlfriend could be angry enough; the bootleggers, car strippers, and bike thieves could be mean enough, scared enough, *and* desperate enough, so I don't know yet. We know the Barnes family, Ray Urdenbach, Mr. Alderson, and the girlfriends—especially Miss Tuley—could be suspects, but..." I grimaced.

"There are two other possibilities."

"Two? Who's the first?"

"My teacher's husband."

"Oh, Nate. Mr. McAllister? That couldn't be. Why would you think that?"

"Well, I heard he lost his job a few weeks ago, then left for Raleigh, so he's located where the car strippers are located and maybe where the bike thieves are located. I mean, who would know better than a teacher when a kid has a new bike?"

"Oh, I don't know, Nate. I can't imagine anyone killing someone to keep from being nabbed for stealing bicycles."

"I can't imagine that either, but maybe he didn't intend to kill him. You know, in the movies, sometimes someone knocks someone out, then someone else comes along with a motive and kills them. Then it looks like the first person killed them."

"I don't even want to think about that. I like Mrs. McAllister. Who is number two?"

"Don't forget Looper Heister—the guy who shot the chief. He could be bootlegging again, and Officer Lum could have been onto him."

"Oh, yeah. I had forgotten about him. You're right; he could be a suspect."

"He's on my list." I leaned toward her.

"By the way, did the coroner say what could have caused that trauma to his neck?"

"A blunt instrument, which could include a pipe, baseball bat, or something like that."

"Or a karate chop? I mean, they break boards, right?"

She nodded. "Yes, I guess so, but I don't want to label that girl in Fayetteville, Jean Ann Tuley, a murderer just yet."

"She has the means—her lethal hands—and she acted like a suspect today when she said she wouldn't be at the funeral."

"But she's still upset, Nate. She liked the guy; maybe she was in love with the guy. She just wasn't ready to watch him get buried." She shook her head. "But she may still be there for the funeral, or at least she may still come over for an interview with Dan. He didn't like her canceling today, so he called her back and told her to be here Wednesday afternoon or he would come and get her."

"Okay. That's good."

"I guess so, but I still don't want to think she was involved; she sounded so sweet on the phone and…well, no motive."

"That we know of."

"True, none that we know of, but Dan's going over to Fayetteville tomorrow to poke around and see what he can find out about her. He's suspicious too."

"Will you tell me what he finds out?"

"We'll see."

Ah, geez, the dreaded "We'll see" again.

"Okay, Mom, at the office today, we never got around to fingerprints. Were there any prints on those burger wrappers I found? Or anything else?"

"There were prints on the wrappers, but whoever they belonged to had never been fingerprinted, so we couldn't get a match."

"Any others? Prints on his neck, maybe?"

"No, he was wearing a scarf—cold night, remember?"

"So, he was clubbed or chopped then strangled through the scarf?"

"Yes. Or with the scarf."

"You don't know if it was from hands or scarf?"

"Dan might know, but he hasn't said."

"Ah...okay, was there anything in his pockets that might have had prints other than his own?"

"No, the body was picked clean."

"Like he was robbed?"

"Could be. Or to remove evidence."

"Has Detective Lewis ruled out robbery?"

"I don't think so. I don't think he's ruled out anything yet."

"He seemed pretty sure about Rachel not being a suspect, so he's ruled her out."

"There's a reason for that."

I opened my mouth to say something, but she held out her palm.

"That's all I'm going to say. You'll just have to wait. And remember, you're not to mention who we suspect or don't suspect to anyone, not even Charlie. Copy that?"

I glanced down. "Yes, ma'am. Solid copy."

I raised my head. "But one more question, please?"

"That depends."

"Do you know *where* he was killed?"

"Dan hasn't said, but he did say he recognized that army blanket he was wrapped in as the one Gunner kept in the trunk of his car, so he must have been near his car when he was killed."

"His personal car, right? The blue Chevy. Not the patrol car."

"Correct."

"Has the car been located? If so, where?"

"That's questions number two and number three."

"So, you're not going to answer?"

"I can answer both by saying I don't know, but that's it."

"And he left to go on vacation Friday, right? The day he was killed."

She grinned. "That's question number four, Nate."

"I'll take that as a 'yes.' I mean, that's what you told us in the car Saturday morning."

"Did I say that?"

"Something like that."

She shook her head. "Okay, enough."

"You don't want to know about Mr. Alderson, the man with all the speeding and parking tickets?"

"Alderson? Oh yeah. What about him?"

"My sources say he doesn't like cops. And Buddy Alderson, his son, the fifth grader, made a big fuss over Jimmy Rayburn's bike the day before it was stolen."

She cocked her head.

"Again, who would kill over a bicycle? But that is suspicious."

She slapped her thighs and stood.

"Okay, that's enough detective talk. Now, let's talk about your social calendar for the rest of the week. You've got the dance on Thursday, the twenty-second, then the basketball game on Friday, the twenty-third, right?"

I stood. "Yes, ma'am."

"Do you want remedial dance lessons before you go?"

"No...I'll just fake it. I'll get by."

"And for the dance…The Shonkasabes are driving?"

"They are for now, but Mr. Shonkasabe wants to go to the basketball game Friday, so he might want to change the dates with you."

"Well, I couldn't do Friday."

"No? Why not?"

She straightened and grinned.

"Dan's invited me to go out with him Friday night. There's a restaurant in Aberdeen he wants to try."

"Ohhh, Mom's got a date, huh?"

She lowered her head and looked at the floor.

"It's no big deal. Just dinner."

"Yeah, right, just dinner."

She looked up, and there was a red tint to her cheeks.

"Hush. Next, you'll tell me to be home by midnight."

"No, ma'am. I was thinking be home by ten."

"I was planning to be home by ten! You kids will be back by then, and we can have hot chocolate and cookies together."

"Hey, good idea. If you loosen him up with hot chocolate and cookies, say by the fire with the Christmas tree lights in full glow, he might tell me where Officer Lum was killed."

Her dimples deepened. "He might. We'll see."

Arghhh.

She hugged me. "Study time."

"Yes, ma'am, back to the world of fractions—my kryptonite."

She walked to the door.

"Becky could help, you know. She's good at math and algebra."

"I'd rather fall on my sword than ask her for help. I'll call Tom Ray and see if he can go over this with me tomorrow."

"Tom Ray Urdenbach? Okay, good luck." She stepped out and closed the door."

Later, I did call Tom Ray, but no one answered.

The next morning broke clear and crisp again, but even with numb hands, the paper route went well. When I threw the paper at the Urdenbachs' the lights were on, so I expected to see Tom Ray in class. The Aldersons, the family that didn't like cops, did not take my paper, but their neighbor did, so when I pedaled by the Aldersons', I noticed their lights were out, and their car was not in the driveway.

When I got to class, the Fryfogel twins, Big Fry and Little Fry stood by the last window on the far side of the room, surrounded by the early arrivals—all talking at the same time. I dropped my books on my desk in the middle of the fourth row and listened.

Apparently, in answer to someone's question, Big Fry said, "Heck, I don't know!"

Billy "Howdy Doody" Westley, who stood between Little Fry and Chipper, looked at Little Fry.

"Did you call the cops?"

Little Fry, the petite blonde with the Tinkerbell ponytail, looked up at him and slammed her hands to her hips.

"Of course, we called the cops, stupid! But it was six o'clock in the morning when Daddy noticed the car was missing, and no one answered the phone!"

Billy scoffed. "Then you call Chief McDonald, *stupid*! Wake him up!"

"Well...I'm sure Daddy did that. We had to get ready for school."

He grinned. "And the chief showed up?"

Big Fry, the biggest guy in the class behind Tom Ray, probably sensing his twin sister had gotten in over her head, pushed his horn-rimmed glasses tight against his face and stepped up to Billy.

"The chief is probably there now, wise guy. Back off."

Billy grinned and took his seat.

"I can't wait to hear about it."

Big Fry took his seat behind Billy.

"Oh, you'll hear about it, Billy. Count on it."

Mrs. McAllister entered in a green coat over a light-blue print dress. As she set her tattered book bag on her desk, the bell rang. Chipper rushed over and dropped onto her seat in front of Charlie's empty desk. She turned, nodded to Charlie's desk, and gave me a look like, *Where's Charlie?*

I shrugged.

I looked over at Tom Ray's desk in the far-right rear corner, which was also empty. *Rats.*

Then, just as Mrs. Mac turned and stepped toward the open door, Charlie slipped in.

From seats two and three in the front row, Rose and Donna chanted, "Charlie's late, Charlie's late!"

Susie Wilkerson, in seat number one of the front row, smiled at Charlie, swung her brown ponytail around, and followed him with an adoring gaze in her doe eyes.

Charlie took his seat in the row beside me. He slipped his

books under the desktop, pushed his hair over his ears, then leaned over.

"Hey, I saw the cops at the Fryfogels' house."

I leaned toward him.

"Yeah, somebody swiped their car."

"No lie?"

"Okay, boys, be quiet back there. Everyone, get out your science—"

The door opened, and Tom Ray, head down, stepped in, closed the door, then strolled back to his desk.

Phew! I'd catch up with him at recess.

Chapter 7

A RING WITH TWO BRANCHES

At recess, I found Tom Ray in the corner of the playground, seated under a naked maple tree. He sat with his watch cap pulled down over his dirty-blond eyebrows and his arms holding his legs against his body. He heard me coming and looked up.

"What do you want?"

I stopped and sat Indian-style in front of him.

"I want to help."

"Help with what?"

"You didn't turn in a history essay."

"So what?"

"So, you're not going to get promoted, man. You want to get out of this childish sixth grade, right?"

"Yeah, but I don't write essays. Mrs. Mac knows that; she set me up."

"Tom Ray, nobody wants you out of that class more than Mrs. Mac. And nobody wants you to succeed more than Mrs. Mac. Well, except me. I want to see you move up to where you belong. You're smart; you can easily handle seventh grade."

He hung his head. "Seventh grade. Big deal."

"But that's just the next step. By the time school is out in June, you could be promoted to eighth grade, and by this time next year, you could be promoted to ninth grade with the other kids your age."

I held out my hands.

"Look, you were tardy. She's got to report that. That's problem number one. You didn't turn in an essay; that's problem number two. Either will keep you from moving up after the Christmas break, whether here or somewhere else."

I pointed at him. "Here's my plan…"

"Look, Nate…You don't get it." He locked his ice-blue eyes on me. "I don't care."

I ignored him and pulled a notepad and pencil from my coat pocket. I held it out to him.

"Write her a note. I'll dictate it to you. Something like, *we're moving; the house is a mess. I've been helping my mother pack, that's why I was late. I forgot to bring the essay. I'll run home at lunch and get it. Please excuse me.*"

"But I didn't write the essay."

"But you will. At lunch. I'll dictate that to you as well. You'll write the glorious story of the founding of the United States Marine Corps, a subject of which I am intimately familiar."

And that's what we did, and believe it or not, we got away with it. So, at least for the time being, and with one more day to go, Tom Ray was still moving up.

I also got a chance to confirm his father was back in his life and wanted Tom Ray and his mother to join him in Raleigh.

Tom Ray, on the weekends, would be helping him with the new landscaping contract he'd gotten. I just hoped that was all he would be helping him with.

After school, as Charlie pulled his bike from the bike rack, I told him I would check in with Mr. Barrow to see what he'd learned at his car dealers association meeting.

He said, "I thought you were going Christmas shopping with your mom."

"I am, but then I'm going to see Mr. Barrow at dusk, so I can watch for Ollie. Remember Ollie, his pet wild owl?"

"Sure, Ollie, the mouse connoisseur."

He mounted up.

"Okay, I'll talk with my neighbor in the argyle socks and see what's going on with the landscapers and confirm the head guy really is Tom Ray's father. I can't wait to find out why they suddenly bailed out Saturday, or at least what excuse they gave. I'll call you tonight."

He pedaled off.

Tom Ray walked up, and I joined him for the walk to his house and my math lesson. On the way, I noticed his bruise was hardly noticeable, and his left eye was totally clear. When we got there, we sat on the top step of his porch in front of a moldy sofa and a rusted-out washing machine (their usual porch décor, another word I'd learned from Charlie).

Over the next ten minutes, Tom Ray tried to straighten me out on the power of the common denominator. That stuff was as easy for him as it was frustrating for me, but I felt more confident about passing that math test the next day. When I stood to go, he looked up and hesitated as if he wanted to add something, but then he looked back down at his Converse high-tops and gave me one of those halfhearted go-ahead waves.

As I walked home anticipating a visit to Mr. Barrow that evening, I also felt more confident about nailing down our suspects. But first, Superman needed some attention, and then all of us, including my beloved sister, would be off on our annual Christmas shopping spree, which, as it turned out, included a couple of surprise sightings.

Every Christmas, Mom and Dad, then Mom, would give us ten dollars each to shop for family and friends. After Mammy passed away, that left my shopping list for the current year at three adults, counting Mrs. Mac, one student in my class, and one very nauseating teenager. The student gifts would be collected in class, numbered, then each student would draw a number from a hat. The limit was twenty-five cents, so that wasn't a significant threat to my budget. The Becky gift would be the challenge. For the Christmas at hand, she considered herself a woman. What does one buy a faux (got that word from Charlie too) woman? Perfume? No. If I'd bought her perfume, she'd have had the house smelling like gardenias or something.

Mom had arrived home from work early, so while I sat on the sofa in the living room and waited for her to announce our takeoff time, I mulled over my shopping list and admired our work on the Christmas tree. Becky stayed in her room while a Frank Sinatra Christmas song played on the radio. Granddaddy waited for us in his workshop. Finally, Mom, in her favorite red-and-white Christmas sweater, returned from the kitchen.

She made a "follow me" motion and said, "Time to launch."

And launch we did, but before we could go downtown, we had to divert the flight a few blocks over to Gill's house on Vermont so Becky could have a look. Alas, "no joy" on Gill.

Pace's Department Store on Broad Street was Christmas shopping central and always a Christmas adventure. With Bing Crosby singing Christmas carols in the background, I wove and slithered through the crowd to the toy section, where I popped open the grocery bag I'd brought from home. I bagged a tube of pickup sticks for the student gift, then moved on to the men's section and the sock rack. Granddaddy wore white cotton socks that came in a plastic package with a locomotive on the front, so I bagged a few packages for him.

I pressed on to the women's section where I bumped, literally bumped, into Chipper.

"Hey, Mary Elizabeth. You shopping for me?"

She laughed and pointed at the loaded shopping basket in her hand.

"Not unless you want nylon stockings. What shade would you like?"

I grinned. "Something in a manly tan, please."

She shook her head.

"Nah, Nate, tan's not your color." She leaned in.

"Hey, what'd you get Mrs. Mac?"

"Gee, I don't know what to do about that. Jimmy said she needed cash."

"No, she doesn't. I heard that rumor too, but she's fine. Her husband is an accountant and only lost his job because the plumbing supply company he worked for in Aberdeen closed down. He just got hired at the Pinehurst Country Club in their accounting department."

"For sure?"

"Yeah, for sure. No problem."

"Okay, that's good news."

A big, smelly, unshaven old man in a soiled denim coat and faded red ball cap tried to wedge his way between us. I grabbed Chipper's arm and pulled her out of his way. He passed us, pushed the guy ahead of him aside with a growl, then walked on toward the back. The crowd flowed in behind him.

After he passed, Chipper wrinkled her nose, waved her hand in front of her face, and watched him walk away. "Wow. Did you smell that?"

"Yeah, smelled like he's missed a few Saturday baths."

"Sure does."

She looked back at me. "You know who that was, don't you?"

"No. Attila the Hun, maybe?"

"Close. That was Mr. Buster Barnes."

"Buster Barnes? You sure?"

"Yes, I'm sure. My father has the insurance policy on his property, and he's described him and that grimy red cap to me often enough—usually in terms of 'Stay away from that guy *and* his family. They're crude, mean, bad-tempered people.'"

I watched him disappear out the rear emergency exit.

"Your dad wouldn't have to tell me twice. Hey…"

I pointed at the red light that came on above the door when it opened.

"He shouldn't be using that rear door for an exit, should he?"

"Certainly not, but who's going to tell him?"

"I don't know."

I stared at the door, then a large woman in a floppy blue hat with a plastic fruit arrangement on top squeezed past us and dragged a small child behind her. The child, a little dark-haired girl in a red dress, smiled at us, and we smiled back.

I looked at Chipper.

"Hey, any more news on the mur—"

I glanced at the next wave of people shuffling past us and whispered, "The case?"

"I was going to ask you the same thing. Rachel will be at the funeral tomorrow; I know that much."

"How's she been taking it?"

"Patty says she's taking it pretty hard." She leaned in closer.

"She said Rachel feels responsible for his death, but she didn't know why—says Rachel has clammed up and only comes out of her room to eat and go to school."

"Suppose it has something to do with the Barnes family?"

"I asked her that, but she didn't know. She also didn't think they were mad enough at Officer Lum to go that far."

She glanced around, then leaned in again.

"But she said they're sure glad he's dead."

"I'll bet they are."

She nodded. "Me too."

"Well, how about asking Patty where Junior and Buster Barnes were last Friday, especially Friday evening. I'm pretty

THE CHRISTMAS TREE CORPSE

sure Jasper Barnes was at the Christmas tree farm, but you might also ask her about him."

"I'll ask, but I don't think she'd know. They're like her step uncles, so she only knows what she overhears from her parents."

"Oh. Okay."

She grinned. "Hey…how 'bout black fishnet stockings for you?"

I grimaced and shook my head. "How 'bout you forgetting I ever brought it up?"

She raised her dark eyebrows at me. "If you insist."

"I insist. Now, back to Mrs. Mac…"

She pointed across the aisle at a shelf with women's scarves.

"Something like a scarf would be good."

"A scarf it is."

"And make it green to go with her coat."

"Green scarf. Got it. Thanks."

"Oops." She pointed a couple of rows over. "There's Mom. Time to go."

From behind a display of women's unmentionables, her mom, in a brown leather coat, stood on her tiptoes like a blonde momma bear looking for her cub.

Chipper waved to her, stepped that way, and then stopped and looked back.

"See you tomorrow. And Thursday night! Don't forget Thursday night!"

I locked my hands in front of me, looked down, and twisted my body like Bashful in *Snow White and the Seven Dwarfs*.

"Ah gosh, Mary Elizabeth, I won't."

She snickered and waved at me like, *Get outta here.*

I watched her join her mom and wave goodbye, and then I wove across the aisle and through the flow of bundled-up people toting shopping bags.

In the next row, I flipped through a few scarves until I came to a green one and bagged it. It had blue polka dots, so I figured it would go with her glasses. At the far end of the row, a sign read, "Dressing Table Accessories." *Perfect.* I wove my way down there and got Becky a mirror, one of those with a magnified side that could magnify pimples.

For Mom, I got a large bottle of Jergens Lotion, her favorite hand cream, and a hair brush with a wooden handle.

I had my whole list checked off except for Superman. For him, I'd have to go to the hardware store. I was thinking of some treats that would be good for his coat. The lad's coat, especially the cowlick, had been looking dull lately.

By the time I got through the checkout line, Mom, Granddaddy, and Becky were already outside in the fading twilight, waiting for me. Mom and Granddaddy stood in front of the car on the edge of the busy sidewalk while Becky stood on the car's bumper. She balanced herself with her hands on Granddaddy's shoulders and stared up the street toward the corner drug store and soda shop.

I got Mom's attention and nodded at Becky. "What's with Becky?"

She grinned. "Oh, she thinks she saw Gill go into the soda shop."

As Becky climbed down, an older man in a baggy tweed sport coat, yellowed white shirt, and a soiled green tie limped past us like his feet hurt. After he passed, Mom elbowed me and nodded toward him.

"Looper Heister."

"Really?"

She nodded. "Doesn't look that dangerous, does he?"

"No, he doesn't."

"Well, looks can be deceiving. According to his criminal record, he's very dangerous."

She turned and stepped over to the car door.

"Return to base, people. RTB."

All the way home, Becky teased me about me talking with my "girlfriend."

I ignored her, which always irritated the heck out of her.

At home, after promising Mom I'd be back by six, I jumped on my bike and pedaled off to Mr. Barrow's house with fingers crossed that I hadn't missed Ollie's evening flight.

Good ol' Wickers opened the door and said, "Good evening, Master Nathan."

On the widow's walk, I found Mr. Barrow bundled up in his wool overcoat and *Sergeant Preston of the Yukon* fur cap. He offered me his binoculars and pointed to the empty top limb of Ollie's favorite pine tree.

"He's already made one pass at something and missed. A second ago, he dove again. I don't know what he has on his menu tonight, but whatever it is has evaded him so far."

He pointed. "Ah, here he comes, back to the tree, empty-handed again."

Ollie, a dark shadow against the gray dusk, lit in the top

of the tree. Once steadied, his head swiveled around as if he wanted to make sure no one had noticed his failure.

I lowered the glasses. "What do you suppose he's after?"

"I don't know, but it could be a young rabbit. Wild rabbits breed all year long, you know, and it's not unusual for them to have a litter in November or December."

"How would a little rabbit defend itself against an owl— especially an owl that big?"

"Guile and quickness are their only defense, but they don't usually stray far from their burrows, their living rooms, so to speak. When threatened, they scurry back down their tunnels into the burrow, which has multiple entrances and exits. The whole complex is called a warren."

He pointed at Ollie. "Ollie has to guess where those exits are and which one they will use next. Don't worry. Those rabbits don't make it easy for the predator."

He smiled. "But keep in mind, if it weren't for Ollie and others like him, we'd be overrun by rabbits and mice."

"I guess so."

I put the glasses back to my eyes. Ollie had his head turned ninety degrees toward us and tilted down. His wings suddenly shot out to their six-foot span, and he dove for the ground.

"There he goes."

A few seconds later, he flew inside the tree with something small in his beak, like a field mouse.

"Looks like he's had to settle for another mouse meal." I handed the glasses to Mr. Barrow. "That was fun."

He took the glasses, and I put my hands in the pockets of my windbreaker.

"Mr. Barrow, do you have time to tell me about your visit to Raleigh?"

"I do, and I've got some news I think you'll want to hear."

He held his hand toward his two-man elevator in the wall behind us.

"Let's go down by the fire and warm up."

Downstairs, I sat in front of the fire in the leather chair beside the table with the Tiffany lamp. Mr. Barrow reclined in his leather rocker on the other side of the table. Wickers entered and served hot chocolate, hot tea, and sugar cookies. I snugged myself into the back of the chair to the squeak of fine leather. Ah…I felt like a favored knight in the king's castle.

Mr. Barrow pulled a cigar from his maroon robe pocket.

"Nate, the buzz at the meeting was all about these car thieves and car strippers. They've been a plague to every dealer across the state—not as much to their new cars as to their used cars. Several dealers have hired security guards to watch their lots at night."

He held out his cigar for Wickers to clip and light it. He took a puff and added, "That can get expensive."

"Was the Barnes family mentioned?" I blew on my hot chocolate and took a sip.

"Yes, they were. Also, several others, including Looper Heister, also known as 'Rabbit,' and your friend's father, Ray Urdenbach."

He took a puff and blew it toward the paneled ceiling.

"And there was a name that surprised me—Mick Alderson." He looked at me.

"Do you know him or of him?"

Wow.

"Yes, sir. He and his family live on East Maine, and I know he doesn't like cops."

"It was just speculation, but his name came up in regard to people from Southern Pines who had been seen with the people my contacts suspected of being involved. It was more like guilt by association than by any evidence of guilt."

He broke off a piece of sugar cookie.

"I was told Alderson used to work for a used car dealer in Raleigh and left under suspicious circumstances."

"And he's back working in Raleigh?"

"No, he's here." He chewed and swallowed his piece of cookie.

"I believe he's a mechanic at the Ford dealership in Aberdeen. But he visits Raleigh."

"Then he stays on my list. How about Mr. Urdenbach? Any solid evidence that he's involved?"

"No, and that's the problem, you see. There isn't any hard evidence against anyone."

He winked. "But plans are being made to correct that."

I swallowed a bite of cookie and chased it with a sip of hot chocolate.

"Just how does this car-stealing, car-stripping thing work anyhow?

"There is a network of spies—I guess that's the best way to describe them. These spies, for a commission on the items stolen, are contacted by the thieves, told what car the thieves need, then the spies alert the thieves when such a car is located."

He snapped off another piece of cookie.

"The thieves steal the car, then either sell it out of state or strip it for parts, or sometimes they repaint it, modify it, and sell it in the state."

He chewed the cookie and then sipped his tea.

"Now, let's say you want a certain model car, but it doesn't come with the transmission you want. *But* you have connections to this organization, this ring of thieves if you will. You go to them, make a down payment, then wait for them to steal, modify, and repaint someone else's car to make it yours with the transmission you want."

"Huh. Well, someone must have wanted a fifty-five yellow Buick Roadmaster because the Fryfogels had theirs stolen last night."

He shook his head. "They're here in our little town. Undoubtedly."

He raised a finger. "And my finger points at that Alderson fella. As you said, he lives in town. Ray Urdenbach lives in Raleigh, and the Barnes family lives out Morganton Road."

"How about Mr. Heister?"

"Rabbit lives north of town and off the Carthage Road. His name did come up in Raleigh, but not as a major player."

Wickers appeared out of the shadows. "If I may, sir."

Mr. Barrows looked up. "Yes, Wickers. What is it?"

"An interjection, sir. Pertaining to Mr. Alderson."

"Certainly, Wickers. Please contribute whatever you can."

Wickers cleared his throat.

"Well, sir, at the Pudgy Pig the other day…At the butcher's counter, to be precise…I happened to overhear an altercation.

For certainly, that's what it would be called, sir. Harsh words were exchanged. The exchange was between the butcher, sir, and Mr. Alderson."

Wickers straightened.

"Yes, Wickers. Go on.

"Yes, sir. It was over a late butcher's bill. A delinquent account would be the term, I believe, sir."

"And was the account settled?"

"No, sir, and Mr. Alderson didn't get his pork chops either, sir."

"I see. Wickers, would you conclude from what you overheard that Mr. Alderson is in arrears and could not settle his account because he is in a period of financial embarrassment?"

"Precisely, sir."

"And he may engage in illegal activity to alleviate that financial situation?"

"Exactly, sir."

Mr. Barrow looked at me. "Does that fit with your knowledge of Mr. Alderson, Nate?"

I looked at Wickers and back to Mr. Barrow.

"Well, yes, sir, it does. I don't know anything about their financial situation, but from what I've heard, the Aldersons are not one of Southern Pines' finest families. Plus, you just said your friends in Raleigh linked him to people they suspect."

He offered a contemplating nod. "Yes…They certainly did."

"Will that be all, sir?"

Mr. Barrow looked up. "Yes, yes, of course, Wickers. Thank you."

"Very good, sir."

I checked my Timex and stood. "I've got to get home, Mr. Barrow—supper time."

He pushed on his cane and stood.

"Wickers will show you to the door, Nate. I've stiffened up again in this cold weather."

He swapped the cane to his left hand and put his right hand on my shoulder.

"But one more little bit of information before you go."

"Yes, sir."

"My friends in Raleigh have reason to believe the bicycle thieves and the car thieves are all connected and part of the same ring—a ring with two branches, if you will."

I looked up as Wickers silently appeared again, then back to Mr. Barrow.

"You mean kids could be involved as well as adults—someone in my school for example?"

"Someone in your school? Yes, perhaps. But it doesn't have to be a student."

Chapter 8

A FUNERAL WITH GIRLFRIENDS

I got home in time for supper, which included supper with Detective Lewis, followed by our monthly game of Clue, which did not include Becky. She was "too cool for Clue."

After supper, while my Professor Plum token was in the study with the Miss Scarlet token, and Becky talked on the phone in the kitchen with Jenny, and Nat King Cole sang Christmas carols in the background, and a fire crackled away in the fireplace, and the bubble lights on the tree bubbled away…the light bulb in my brain came on.

In the game of Clue, unlike what I was dealing with in the Lum murder, the players had to figure out who did it, where they did it, and what instrument of death was used to do it, but not why they did it. We had the possible why or motive for all of our suspects in the Lum murder except one.

I looked over the coffee table at Detective Lewis seated on the floor like me. His Mr. Green token sat in the kitchen with the Colonel Mustard token and the miniature knife.

"Detective Lewis, all our suspects have a motive except Miss Tuley. What do we know about her?"

Lewis, in a green V-neck sweater over a white shirt, looked at Mom, who wore a brown dress and pearls for the occasion and was seated on the sofa with Grandaddy. She looked back at him with a shy grin like, *I told you he was going to prod you for information.*

He rolled the die, got a two, and decided to take the secret passage to join me in the study. He plopped his Mr. Green token between my Professor Plum and the miniature rope and looked at me with a suspicious glare.

"I suspect Nate, in the study, with the rope, of asking too many questions."

I shrugged. "Well, geez. You can't blame a fella for trying."

He smiled. "No, you can't, but I can't tell you what I don't know either. First of all, she's not really a suspect. I've only talked with her twice, and both were brief conversations with an invitation to visit with me. I just asked her to help me fill in some blanks about the case. She agreed, refused in a conversation with your mother, then agreed again after I talked with her the second time. I'll get a chance to do a full interview with her tomorrow after the funeral. After that, she may be a suspect, but for now, I just hope she can help us with information."

"Then will you tell me what she says? And what Miss Creech says?"

"Maybe."

"Ah, come on, Detective Lewis. Only 'maybe'?"

"Yes, but that's a definite maybe."

"Oh, yes, sir, a definite maybe."

I shook my head. "Okay, if you definitely maybe tell me

what you know about Miss Tuley and Miss Creech, I'll definitely maybe tell you what I know about Mr. Alderson, *and* I'll tell you about who killed who in high school."

"Humm…I don't know of any high school murders."

"It's a cold case from years ago, but it could be connected to Officer Lum's murder."

"Years ago, huh? Well, we'll see."

Arghhh. I gave my head a twitch as if to shake off another rejection.

"Okay, then how about Looper Heister? Have you talked with him yet? And by the way, did you know his nickname was 'Rabbit'?"

"Rabbit, huh? No, I didn't know that. I spoke with him this morning about his alleged bootlegging activities, but I intentionally didn't mention the murder. He wasn't very cooperative, plus he had an alibi for last Friday afternoon and evening."

"Have you ruled him out?"

"No, not yet, but his alibi was pretty solid—not perfect, but solid enough to put him on the back burner for now."

"What was his ali—"

Mom held up her hand.

"Nate, please…leave Dan alone, and let's get on with the game."

Lewis looked at his watch.

"It's okay, Connie. I've got to go back to the office anyhow, so let's pause the game here and pick it up again next time."

He stood, and Mom stood with him. She touched his arm.

"Is that the meeting with the you-know-who you told me about this morning?"

"Yep, that's the guy."

He walked toward the door. Mom followed.

"Oh, good. Can't wait to hear about it."

He picked up his fedora from the table, then opened the door.

"Tune in tomorrow at eight for all the details."

"I'll be there." She waved goodbye and shut the door.

As she walked over to the fireplace, I looked up at her from my cushion on the floor.

"The 'you-know-who?' Okay, Mom, what's up?"

Granddaddy, still in his green army sweater and jeans, laid his arm on the back of the sofa and propped his slipper-clad feet on the coffee table.

"Yeah, let's have it, Connie. Who's the 'you-know-who' at the 'you-know-where' in the 'you-know-what' situation?"

She stopped and stood with her back to the fire and hands clasped behind her.

"Sorry, boys. Police business."

"A hint, Mom, please. A hint couldn't hurt."

"I know you guys—a hint would lead to the whole story."

"We're family, Mom. We're not reporters for the *Raleigh News*. Come on…Who is this guy he's meeting?"

Granddaddy coughed onto the crook of his arm. "And why?"

"If Dan tells me I can tell you, I'll tell you tomorrow. For now, I'll just say he's from Raleigh, and that's all I'm going to say."

She pointed at me. "I think someone has some homework to do and a paper route in the morning and should probably be getting it done, then getting to bed."

I stood. "Is he here about Officer Lum's murder?"

She crouched and stalked toward me like a gorilla.

"Yes, but go now, Nathan Hawke, or I'll tear you from limb to limb."

I crashed into her with a hug. "Okay, okay. I'm gone."

She hugged me back and then patted down my cowlick.

"I'll come and tuck you in when you're ready."

As I left, Granddaddy stood, and I heard him say, "Well, my precious but secretive daughter, I'll be in my workshop."

He paused, then added, "Knock if you want to unload any of those heavy secrets you have weighing on you, like why you have that police journal on the floorboard of your car."

I turned as Mom slapped her hand to her forehead and ran for the dining room.

"Oh, shhh...sugar!"

With the bottom of her dress billowing out behind her, she turned left at the dining room and then into the kitchen. I heard the backdoor open, and her black pumps hit the step.

Hmm...police journal.

In the dark the next morning, Wednesday the twenty-first, I left the house all bundled up in my wool coat, red scarf, and blue baseball cap. The air was cold enough to chill my nose and toes but not cold enough to keep me from searching Mom's car for that police journal. I didn't find it on or under the seats, so I figured she had locked it in the glove compartment or the trunk...or she had it with her in the room she shared with Becky.

Granddaddy had the extra car keys and usually kept them in the dresser's top drawer, the one on the right side of the room between the door and the closet. I walked back inside.

At the dresser, I loosened my scarf and then eased the top drawer open to the faint scraping of wood on wood. I only had it out a few inches when I heard Granddaddy cough. I snapped my head around. He lay in his baggy blue-and-white striped pajamas with his eyes open and his hands behind his head on his pillow. He pointed.

"They're in the front left-hand corner."

"Sir?"

"The car keys are in the front left-hand corner of the drawer."

"Oh."

"And I thought I heard the trunk slam last night after she went out, so I'd look there first." He grinned. "But if you learn anything, I expect you to tell me about it."

I nodded. "Yes, sir, you bet."

I pulled out the drawer, lifted a stack of thin, well-worn white railroad socks, and then retrieved the keys. I closed the drawer and turned.

"Got 'em, Granddaddy. Thanks."

He waved and rolled over on his side.

Outside, back in the cold, Superman looked up from his thick bathroom mat inside his cozy doghouse with the green shingled roof. Granddaddy and I had built that for him the year before. As the wrinkles between his eyes deepened, he watched me go by again like, *Even with a paper route, I still think you're crazy for getting up this early.*

At the car and behind the back bumper, I carefully and quietly turned the key in the trunk. It clicked open with a metallic crack like a rifle shot. I snapped my head up and looked around. All quiet, but I pictured Granddaddy on the other side of the brick wall and the bedroom window with a smile on his thin, wrinkled face.

The trunk opened with a creak, the trunk light came on, and there it was—a light-blue, bound journal lying on our plaid picnic blanket. I picked it up and flipped to the last entry.

"Put it back, Nate!"

I turned. Down the driveway, Mom hung out the side window of her bedroom.

"You know what curiosity did to the cat, so put it back and bring me those keys."

Crap, so close.

"Yes, ma'am." I put it back onto the blanket and closed the trunk lid.

The route went well that morning. A light frost covered the ground, so I tried to avoid lawns and just hit walkways and porches. The whole time, the last four words in Lum's journal kept reappearing in my mind: *after the game—park.*

Back at the house, I exercised and watered Superman, then walked to school. I wasn't looking forward to the math test, but I was looking forward to seeing Jimmy Rayburn and Monty "Big Fry" Fryfogel again. I felt sure Jimmy had more to tell me, and I knew Big Fry was on the car-stripping and bootlegging cases. He had promised me he would talk with his cousin in Carthage about Looper Heister.

When the school bell rang at eight, it had warmed into the fifties, and a few scattered clouds had drifted in from the west. Mrs. Mac, in a festive red wool dress and blue polka-dot glasses, stood behind a pile of gifts on her desk.

She quieted us down and then read the morning announcements: "One, no talking in the hallways when going to or from recess—lots of complaints about that from other teachers. Two, high school Christmas dance this evening in the gym does not include junior high, so be sure to get home after school and not loiter around the parking lot or playground. Three, there will be a short band practice after school, and that does include junior high, and four, the Blue Devil basketball team will play Aberdeen at eight tomorrow night, so come and support the team."

She looked up.

"Now. Put your books away and have a sharpened pencil ready."

I looked over at Tom Ray, who shot me a thumbs-up.

As Big Fry, Donna, and Jimmy walked to the table under the first side window to sharpen their pencils at the pencil sharpener, Mrs. Mac removed a pile of mimeographed paper from the side drawer of her desk.

Charlie looked over at me. "Piece of cake, Kemosabe."

I smirked. "I hope so."

Tom Ray had prepared me well, so there weren't any surprises on the test, but still...being mathematically challenged left me unsure of the results.

An hour later, after the test, the teacher's pets, Rose and Donna, collected the papers. Rose made it a point to look at mine and chuckle.

After the girls delivered the papers to Mrs. Mac, she stood.

"I'm going to grade these right now, so while I'm doing that, I want you to *quietly* read chapter sixteen in your history book." She looked at "Howdy Doody" Westley.

"The quieter you are, *Billy*, the faster I can finish the papers and the sooner we can have our party. Do we understand each other, class?"

Billy held up his palms like, *Why me?*

The rest of us said, "Yes, ma'am."

At ten o'clock, with the room in a peaceful calm (Tom Ray was asleep), there was a knock at the door. Mrs. Mac put her red pen down and walked to the door with a smile. When she opened it, Mrs. Chippenvale, the petite blonde, and Mrs. Shonkasabe, the tall, stately brunette, walked in carrying thermos jugs and bags.

The room came alive, and I looked at Charlie. "Chocolate chip cookies?"

He winked. "Hope so."

Chipper turned around. "They're big gingerbread men, boys, and we've made one for each kid in the class."

Charlie leaned forward. "Do you know what's in the jugs Mom's carrying?"

"Hot apple juice with cinnamon and cloves."

"That's right—fresh apple juice, and I crushed the apples." He polished his fingernails on his shirt.

The ladies walked across the front of the room to the tables under the windows while Mrs. Mac walked back to her desk. She turned.

"Give me five more minutes, children, and we'll start the party. Meanwhile, keep your seats and hold down the noise."

She looked at Rose and held out a stack of test papers.

"Rose, honey, please give these out while I finish."

Well, the damage wasn't that bad—a B-, my first B of any kind in math. I shot Tom Ray a thumbs-up.

Big Fry from the row on my left side gave me an "okay" sign and pointed outside. He mouthed, *Recess*.

The gifts were drawn, and the treats consumed. Charlie's gingerbread man had long brown hair, Billy's had red hair, and mine had a cowlick. I got a deck of playing cards, Little Fry (Molly) got my pickup sticks, and Charlie got a Cootie game, which I knew cost more than twenty-five cents. When he unwrapped it, Susie smiled big and clapped. Without expression, Charlie slipped it into his desk.

At recess, I found Jimmy over by the swings talking with Little Fry. I was three steps away from him when I heard footsteps behind me.

"Hey, Nate. Hold up a minute."

I stopped and turned.

Big Fry walked toward me and motioned for me to join him. We met between the swings and the monkey bars.

"What's up, Monty? Hopefully, you learned something in Carthage."

He pushed his horn rims against his face.

"I did. Got some scoop on Looper Heister."

"Great. Let's hear it."

"Okay, my cousin lives just down the road from them, and…"

He poked me.

"Now, get this: His sons still live with him. And they're in their forties!"

"Okay. The scoop, Monty, what's the scoop?"

"Yeah, well, the sons are hardly ever there during the day and not always at night either. My cousin—that's Jake, on my mother's side—said his father, my uncle, thinks the sons are out running a still on Burnt Corn Creek."

"So that's why the sons aren't there every night?"

"That's what Jake said his father thinks, but they were all there last Friday night, and there were lots of cars and trucks there too, like they had a party."

"A party? Did Jake mention music?"

"No, just cars and trucks coming and going and lots of lights on in the house and barn. But here's the weird part: The party, if that's what it was, didn't start until around eleven, and that's why Jake noticed it—all those cars and trucks and a few with busted mufflers going by his house woke him up."

"If they were coming and going and there wasn't any music, I doubt if it was a party. It sounds more like they might have brought in their latest batch of moonshine, and the sale was on."

"Agree, and so does my uncle. He's the Carthage First Baptist minister and does not 'consume nor abide' alcohol."

"Okay, so cousin Jake can confirm that Mr. Heister was at home last Friday night."

"He can confirm his truck was there late Friday night, but

he didn't say he saw Mr. Heister. Actually, he said he didn't see anyone there when he went to bed that evening. That would have been, oh, nine thirty or so."

I scratched behind my ear. "Okay, I don't know who or what Mr. Heister is using for an alibi in the murder case, but if that was a liquor sale going on, I doubt he'd use that."

He poked me again. "What if my uncle called the police to complain, Officer Lum drove out there to arrest them, and they killed him?"

"But he was on vacation last Friday. He wouldn't have been out trying to arrest bootleggers. That's what's screwing up this whole case. He should have been on his way to Charlotte."

The bell rang, and we both turned and walked toward the backdoor to the classrooms. On the way, he poked me again. "If we only knew time of—"

I held up my hand. "I'm right here, Monty. You don't need to poke me."

"Oh, sorry."

After lunch, we spent the rest of the school day discussing chapter 16, which included the massacre of Custer's Seventh Cavalry at the Little Big Horn by the Sioux, Cheyenne, and Arapaho. There was only a brief reference to what the US cavalry did to the Lakota Sioux later at Wounded Knee. Charlie knew that Indian versus US cavalry history very well. On his three-ring binder, he had written, "Custer had it coming."

After school, I walked home with Jimmy Rayburn. When we got to Orchard Road, I turned right, and he continued down Ridge Street toward his house. He hadn't thought of anything else he could tell me, but he said the Aldersons' fifth grader, Buddy, had a new blue bike that looked an awful lot like his stolen red bike.

The burial service for Officer Lum was held that afternoon at four o'clock at Manly Cemetery and, at Mom's request, was conducted by the pastor of our Presbyterian church. Lum's mother and sister were there from Charlotte, and like Officer Lum, they didn't attend any church or have any religious affiliation, so they were happy to have Mom take care of the arrangements.

At the grave site, I sat with Becky in the middle of the second row of folding white chairs. I watched Detective Lewis, in a charcoal suit, white shirt, and gray tie, plus five volunteers from our church, all in dark suits, carry the coffin from the hearse toward the site. Becky kept watching the driveway.

I finally leaned over and whispered, "Who are you looking for?"

"None of your business."

"Oh, must be Gill. Why would Gill be here?"

She blew out a sigh.

"Gill knew Officer Lum was a big basketball fan, never missed a game, so he might be here. Besides, I thought Rachel would be here, and he would come with her."

She nodded toward the young woman at the end of the first row.

"Hey, is that one of the girlfriends—the petite young woman with the long dark hair?"

"If it is, it might be Jean Ann Tuley—petite but fit. Very fit."

"She wears black well." She looked past the sitting area.

"And the young woman standing over there—the short, shapely blonde with the big shoulders?"

"That's probably Elsa Creech from Charlotte. She's a masseuse."

"Yeah, I would have guessed that...or a mud wrestler."

She looked back at Miss Tuley.

"Hmm. He liked them young, and he liked them short."

A minute later, Chief McDonald, Mom, and Detective Lewis sat in front of us with Lum's family, then the service began. The pastor did a nice job of accurately describing Officer Lum's gentle, caring nature, his pride in serving in the US Army, and his pride in serving the people of Southern Pines. Rachel did not show. The girlfriends and Mom, even Becky, shed some tears. I have to admit, I got a little choked up myself, then it was over.

Throughout the service, I kept a wary eye on the girlfriends, but in the end, I couldn't read them one way or the other. If one of them was a killer, she was alley-cat sneaky about it.

As we followed the crowd back to our car, I saw motion inside a grove of tall oak trees to my right, about thirty yards away from the grave site. An average-sized man in a suit and fedora, a very tall woman, and a tall teenage girl in a black dress walked down the slope. The girl dabbed her eyes with a white handkerchief. They stopped at a wooden-sided station wagon on the side of the cemetery driveway. I grabbed Becky's arm and nodded toward the station wagon.

"Is that Rachel?"

She looked, shrugged, and said, "Can't see her that well. Could be."

"I think that's her. I was told she would be here. Maybe Officer Lum just liked girls—short or tall."

On the drive home, and out of frustration from not being fully included in the information loop, I decided it was time to take action, time to get aggressive, and I knew where to start.

Chapter 9

KIDNAPPED

The night after the funeral, I went to bed excited about only having to wait three more days and a wake-up for my pump BB gun, but I lay sleepless due to frustration. Mom still wouldn't tell me who the "you-know-who" was, what was in the journal, or what Lewis found out from Miss Tuley and Miss Creech. She wouldn't budge even when I told her I had information on Looper Heister's Friday night. So, I came up with a plan, an aggressive plan. After convincing myself the plan would work, I finally fell asleep.

The next morning, December 22, arrived with warmer temperatures, more humid air, and wet ground from an overnight shower. It was still chilly, so I pedaled my route in a thin sweater, ball cap, and tan windbreaker. Overhead, thick gray clouds hung in the sky. At the end of the route and on a hunch, I did a slow fly-by at the Aldersons' place. Sure enough—a new blue bike lay on the porch's deck. Apparently, Buddy Alderson wasn't worried about it being stolen the way Jimmy's bike was stolen. That was all the confirmation I needed. The Aldersons had to be involved in the stolen bike ring.

I also rode by Charlie's house. I knocked on his window, woke him up, asked him to meet me at my house later, and promised him it would be worth it.

At six thirty, as Superman and I roamed the edge of the backyard looking for the tennis ball I'd thrown and he'd ignored, Charlie slid his bike to a stop by the Superman suite. He dismounted and popped his kickstand into place.

As he walked toward us, he tapped his Lone Ranger watch.

"Let the record show I was here at exactly six thirty."

I looked at my watch. "I've got six thirty-one, but...that's close enough."

"You still think this is a good idea? I mean, it better be. The first day of Christmas break, and you've got me here at *six thirty*. That's grounds for criminal charges right there."

"Well, we'll know soon enough. You got cash?"

"You aren't buying? Hey, this was your idea."

"Okay, okay, my treat. Just don't get carried away. Two dollars is the limit."

"No problem. I can eat pretty good on two bucks."

"That's two bucks for both of us, Charlie."

"Oh. Well, a dollar fifty for me will be enough." He pointed at me. "But why do you think we're going to learn anything?"

"That's *one dollar* for you, buffalo breath, and I think we'll learn something because Mrs. Willabee, one of my paper customers, works at Benny's. I think she'll help us. If nothing else, she can tell us who regularly orders hamburgers to go for lunch."

"Oh yeah, the wrappers. Okay then, let's roll."

He walked toward his bike but looked back over his shoulder.

"Hardware store afterward, right? I need to get something for Dad."

"That's the plan."

I called Superman, and we walked to his suite.

"Santa's going to bring you some treats, super dog."

He twisted his head and looked at me like, *I have no idea who Santa is, but I heard the word treat, so as long as I don't have to play that stupid "sit" game with him, I'm in.*

On our way to Benny's Diner at the north end of town, we pedaled by the Aldersons', and I pointed out Buddy's new bike to Charlie. He wanted to stop and examine it for signs it had been repainted, but I convinced him we needed to get to the diner. Men like the Barneses and the Heisters eat early.

We arrived at 6:50 a.m. Two men in jeans, barn coats, and green John Deere caps walked out the door and stopped at a blue pickup truck. As they climbed into the truck's cab, we dismounted and rolled our bikes onto the sidewalk. We parked them by a newspaper rack in front of large windows with fake snow sprayed in the corners and paper snowflakes taped to the glass. I pointed to a rusty red pickup truck pulling out of the parking lot and onto Broad Street.

"Look familiar?"

He nodded. "Mr. Jasper."

"Yep. We missed him."

"That better not mean we don't get to eat."

"No, we eat." I reached over and opened the door for him. "I see a truck in the lot I recognize."

As we stepped in, Tennessee Ernie Ford sang "We Wish You a Merry Christmas" while laughter, the clatter of dishes, and cigarette smoke washed over us.

Inside I noticed an empty booth against the windows in the center of the diner to our left. In the next booth down from the empty booth, a tall man in a leather jacket sat alone with his back to us. A brown, rumpled fedora sat on the back of his head

I nodded toward the empty booth.

"Get that booth for us, Charlie. I'll be right there."

Mrs. Willabee, in a white dress with a red Christmas apron tied around her ample waist, stood behind the cash register. She closed the drawer and then handed some change to a gentleman in a tan corduroy sport coat. He turned and walked toward the door. She patted down her puffed-up bottle-blonde hair, brushed off her apron, then noticed me walking toward her. She smiled and opened her mouth as if to speak, but I held a finger to my lips, and she nodded.

I stepped up and leaned over the counter by the cash register.

"Mrs. Willabee, will you do me a big favor?"

She glanced around the diner, then leaned toward me.

"Sure, sugar. What's up?"

I nodded toward our booth, where Charlie had taken a seat on the side facing us and was pushing his hair back over his ears.

"Who is the guy in the leather jacket with the brown fedora seated behind my friend, Charlie?"

"That's Ray Urdenbach. You know him?"

"No, but I know his son."

"Oh, Tom Ray. Yeah, you know…I really feel for that boy and his mother. They're moving, you know, and I don't think either of them wants to go. Living with Ray can't be easy. Know what I mean?"

"I'm sure it isn't."

I glanced over at Mr. Urdenbach, then back to Mrs. Willabee.

"I want to place an order for Charlie and me, and when you deliver it to us, I want you to make conversation with Mr. Urdenbach—give him his check, or ask him if he wants more coffee or something like that."

She nodded. "Okay."

Just then, a couple walked by, and the man said, "Cash on the table, Mable, and thanks."

She raised and smiled. "Thanks, sugar. Bye, Alma. Hope that grandbaby's okay."

They waved and left.

She leaned toward me.

"Okay, so what should I talk about? You know me. I can talk about anything." She winked. "Know what I mean?"

"Ask him if he has heard about the Officer Lum murder and say something like, I heard they were going to burn that field where the body was found."

"I'm sure he's heard about the murder, sugar. Everybody's heard about that, but I didn't know Jasper was going to burn that field."

"The trees are eaten up with mites, and the whole field was scheduled to burn the day after I found the body, but I'm trying to find out who knew the field would be burned. The murderer must have known, or he—or she—wouldn't have put the body there. They can't burn the field now because it's a crime scene. So, could you kinda find out for me if Mr. Urdenbach knew about the burn *before* I found the body?"

"Oh yeah, that would be the clever thing to do, you know—burn the evidence." She leaned closer. "Hey, are you saying Ray killed Officer Lum?"

"No, no, not at all. I don't know who killed him. I just suspect anyone who knew the field would be burned."

"Yeah, well, burning that field—still clever."

"Yes, it would be clever. By the way, does Mr. Urdenbach know Jasper Barnes?"

"Oh yeah. Jasper was just in here sitting with him. They're regulars, you know."

"Really? Okay, thanks. I'll be in the booth."

She grabbed my arm. "Wait a minute there, junior detective. The order?"

I grinned. "Oh yeah. Two eggs scrambled, grits, bacon crisp, toast dark, and small orange juice for both. With butter and strawberry jam, please."

She winked. "Got it, sugar."

I walked to our booth and slid onto the side facing Charlie and Urdenbach's back. I took off my cap. Not polite to eat while wearing a hat or a cap.

"Grits on their way, Charlie."

He leaned toward me. "I don't get to order for myself? Look, Kemosabe, I want my eggs scrambled, bacon crisp, and toast dark. With butter. And with strawberry jam."

"Well...Tell you what, my faithful friend and companion...That's what I ordered for myself, so you can have my order, and I'll eat the other order."

He scoffed. "Okay, that's better."

Before our order was ready, Mrs. Willabee walked by with another order, and Urdenbach called to her. He held up his coffee cup.

She smiled. "Be right back, sugar."

When she returned with the coffee pot, she poured his coffee and said, "You know what I heard this morning?"

"What?"

"Can you keep a secret?"

"I can, but you obviously can't."

She straightened. "Well, sorry."

He shook his head. "Never mind. What's the secret?"

She leaned closer to him. "Jasper's Christmas tree field has mites."

He scoffed. "Oh hell, Mable, we knew that a week ago. The extension agent from NC State was here. He told us."

He pointed two booths down. "Remember? We sat right over there—heavy guy in khaki clothes and jacket."

"Well, shucks. I thought I had a scoop."

"Not hardly."

He took a sip. "I gotta go. Meet me at the register."

"Okay, sugar."

She walked to the end booth, where another guy held up his cup. From the service window behind the counter, a bell rang, and someone shouted, "Order up!"

Charlie's eyes widened. He leaned toward me to say something, but I shook my head and held out my palm to him. He stopped. Urdenbach, a cigarette hanging from his lips, slid out of his seat. I looked down and pretended to be digging for something in the pocket of my jeans.

As Mr. Urdenbach walked past us, he watched Mrs. Willabee go behind the counter so he didn't notice us. He paid his bill and left without looking our way.

As the door closed behind him, Charlie thumped the table. "He knew!"

"He and probably everyone else who knew Jasper Barnes."

Mrs. Willabee stepped up with a tray holding our orders.

"Okay, sugar, which one of you gets the eggs scrambled?"

Charlie raised his hand. "That's mi—"

She chuckled and slid a plate to Charlie and a plate to me, then set the orange juice and water by the plates.

"Enjoy, boys."

Charlie looked up at her. "Merci beaucoup, madame."

"Tu es le bienvenu, mon ami." She winked and turned back to the counter.

Charlie looked at me and grinned.

"How 'bout that? The lady knows French." He cut into his eggs with his fork.

"You got lucky on this order, Nate."

"Not lucky at all, *mon ami*. You've eaten breakfast with us so many times I knew what you would want. I don't get a thank-you?"

"Thank you. Now…" He swallowed. "He knew, Nate! So, what else would connect him?"

"The landscape guys, I guess."

"But what's his motive? And where was he last Friday evening?"

I swallowed a bite of eggs.

"I don't have a motive…unless he's part of the car-stripping operation Officer Lum was investigating. I think I told you he used to drive for Buster Barnes."

"Hey, maybe Tom Ray would know something."

"He might, but even if he did, would he tell me?"

I scooped some grits and thought of Mammy. She had insisted we eat from everything on the plate and not finish one item at a time. "Not polite," she would say. As I was in Benny's Diner and not in polite company, I didn't think anyone would notice how I did it, but I did it Mammy's way anyhow.

I looked up. Charlie crumbed up his bacon and mixed it in with his grits, which were overflowing with melted butter. I doubted if Mammy would have approved, but as I said…

A hand touched my shoulder. Mrs. Willabee stopped between us with a pitcher of water.

"Got something else for you, Nate. Don't know if it will mean anything, but it might."

"Anything will help, Mrs. Willabee. What is it?"

"Well, I liked Officer Lum, know what I mean? He was always polite and tipped well."

She set the pitcher on the table and glanced around like she wanted to make sure Benny didn't see her.

"He was in here for lunch the day he was murdered."

She stepped closer. Two men in suits walked behind her and took Urdenbach's booth. She leaned over to us.

"He was in here in civilian clothes and with a young woman."

I said, "Was she a young-young woman?"

She nodded. "Long, dark hair. Petite."

Charlie leaned in. "Did you hear a name?"

"No, but they seemed close, you know, like they were on a date. Sat together on the same side of the booth and all."

Charlie scooped up the remains of his grits, so I said, "A lunch date?"

"More like lunch and afternoon date. I heard them talking about Christmas trees—what size to get, stuff like that. I got the feeling it was for her."

"A tree for her, huh?"

"Yeah, they were going to Jasper's after they ate."

Charlie picked up a triangle of toast he had slathered with strawberry jam.

"Was a Fraser fir mentioned?"

"Ah…a type of tree, right?"

We nodded.

"Not sure, but I think so. I think she mentioned Fraser fir." She crossed her arms. "Yeah, she said that was the only real Christmas tree—the Fraser fir."

"Mable!"

Benny, in his white paper cap and full apron, stood in the doorway to the kitchen with his hands on his hips. He rolled his toothpick to the other side of his mouth.

Mrs. Willabee jerked her head around and reached for the order pad in her apron pocket.

"Yeah, Benny, just a minute!"

She tore off our copy of the order and handed it to me.

"Be back in a minute, boys." She leaned over and whispered, "The toothless lion calls."

I looked at the order: $2.26. *I shouldn't have added the orange juice.*

I dug out thirty-five cents from my pocket for Mrs. Willabee, put it on the table, then grabbed my cap.

"Come on, let's mosey."

Charlie chugged his orange juice. "Right behind you."

As we stepped up to the counter, Mrs. Willabee whipped through the kitchen's swinging door. She took my three dollars and hit the cash key with gusto.

"That Benny can be a jerk sometimes, you know what I mean? He wanted to know what you boys were up to."

I glanced at the kitchen door and service window, but no Benny.

"What'd you tell him?"

"I told him you were just playing boy's day out and blowing your paper route money."

I sighed. "Ah, thanks, Mrs. Willabee."

"Glad to do it, sugar."

She winked. "Our talk is our secret. Know what I mean?"

Charlie poked me. "What about the wrappers?"

"Oh yeah." I turned back to Mrs. Willabee.

"Is there anyone who eats lunch here and always has a hamburger to go?"

"Too many to count, sugar, but definitely Jasper Barnes. Lately, he's been eating the special, then taking a burger for himself and one for Gill back to the tree farm."

Behind her, Benny appeared in the service window and slid two plates of food on the shelf. He frowned and hit the bell. "Order up!"

She dropped the change into my outstretched hand and smiled.

"Come back to see me, boys."

On the ride back downtown, with Charlie flipping his long hair back and forth with each stroke of the pedals, he said, "So Mr. Jasper gets burgers to go for lunch. That doesn't really help us does it?"

"No, I guess not. It's his farm; he works there."

"Kinda interesting about Officer Lum and his girlfriend, though."

"Very interesting. And anyone who knew Jasper Barnes knew about the burn."

"Sounds like we didn't rule anyone out. We just added a bunch more in."

"'Fraid so."

Like every store in our little town, the hardware store buzzed with people talking and shopping over a background of cheerful holiday music. I went straight to the pet section while Charlie split for the hand tools. I spent a few minutes reading labels on the selection of treats, then decided to buy the Milk-Bone dog biscuits advertised on the *Rin-Tin-Tin* TV show, plus some beef jerky. As I reached for the Milk-Bone box with the least dents, I smelled something familiar and distasteful—onions and body odor. I looked up.

Jasper Barnes leaned over me. He grabbed the shoulder of

my windbreaker and pulled me to his tobacco-stained overalls and against his bloated gut.

"Ain't you that smart-aleck kid that found that pissant Lum's body on my farm?"

"Ah, sir?"

"That's you, ain't it?"

"I'm just here buying treats for my pit bull, sir. He's outside by my bike."

"You're a smart aleck and a liar, kid. I saw you ride up."

"Oh well, Superman was trailing behind me. You know how male dogs want to pee on every tree. He's out there now, I'm sure."

"Well, let's go see, shall we, wise guy?"

He yanked me off my feet and dragged me stumbling toward the double front door.

"Pit bull, my raw hind end."

I screamed, "Help! Somebody help me! This crazy man is trying to kidnap me!"

The crowd noise died like someone had thrown a switch, but instead of helping me, the people—men, women, and children with shopping bags—just parted like the Red Sea. Barnes dragged me toward the doors and swung his free arm at people as we went. I saw Mr. Mason, the store owner, with a wild look on his face, pick up the phone on the cashier's counter. By then, Barnes had opened the front door on the right side of the double doors.

As he did that, I slipped out of my jacket and took off back into the store, but the crowd had closed behind us, and I bounced off a young woman holding a little boy's hand.

A big, heavy hand grabbed my shoulder and a wad of my sweater.

With "Jingle Bells" now blasting from the speakers, Barnes turned me around, twisted my sweater into a knot, and slapped me across my face.

"Ohhh, kid, you shouldn't have run from Jasper Barmes. Nooo. Nobody runs from—"

His head jerked, his eyes rolled into his head, and he crumpled to the floor like a three-hundred-pound sack of potatoes.

I straightened my cap and stared at him, and then I noticed Charlie standing there with a rubber mallet in his hand.

He tossed it on the floor and looked at me.

"I think it's time we made tracks, Kemosabe."

"Whew! Capital idea. Let's go!"

We ran out onto the sidewalk and dodged a tall police officer in a blue uniform.

He grabbed at us. "Whoa, there, boys. What's going on?"

I tried to get to my bike, but he got there at the same time I did and held it.

"I'm Officer Nettles from Pinehurst, and I'm filling in for Chief McDonald while he's short of staff. Mr. Mason called me. Okay? Understand?"

I braced against my bike and blew out a big, long sigh.

"Oh, yes, sir, am I glad to see you."

He let go of my bike. "What happened?"

"Jasper Barnes tried to kidnap me!" I took another breath. "Charlie hit him with a rubber mallet." I pointed to the front door. "He's on the floor inside."

He looked at Charlie.

"You're Charlie?"

"Yes, sir."

Nettles looked back at me.

"Then you must be Nathan Hawke, Connie's son."

"Yes, sir."

"Well...Nate."

He sighed. "Let me deal with Mr. Barnes first, and then I want to talk with you two again, so don't go away."

He looked at me with sad eyes, like he was about to apologize for something.

"I would have headed this way in a minute to look for you anyhow. I'm afraid I've got some bad news for you, Nate. It's about Detective Lewis."

Chapter 10

LUM'S JOURNAL

After I'd retrieved my windbreaker, Officer Nettles led a woozy Jasper Barnes to the SPPD and booked him for attempted kidnapping and assault. He locked him in one of the two jail cells behind the door on the left side of the police department, dropped the keys into the duty officer's desk drawer, then called Charlie and me into Detective Lewis's office.

We sat in the heavy wooden chairs facing Lewis's desk, and Officer Nettles sat behind the desk in the roller chair. On the coat rack against the wall to our left by the file cabinets, a new SPPD uniform hung from a coat hanger.

Nettles cleared his throat.

"Boys, I'm sorry, but your friend Detective Lewis is in the Moore County Hospital…and he's unconscious. All we know so far is that his car ran off the road last night and hit an oak tree. A passing motorist found him early this morning—still in his car but barely alive. Nate, your mom is with him at the hospital. She asked me to find you and tell you to call her."

I leaned closer. "Where? Where did it happen?"

"Sheldon Road, north of town. He was probably on his way home to that cottage he rents behind the Mannerly farm-house."

He glanced at the notepad on the desk, then back to me.

"That's all we know for now."

Charlie raised his hand.

"Have you been to the scene, or has Chief McDonald been to the scene?"

"I haven't, but based on what the chief told me, he has."

I looked at the city map on the wall behind us.

"How far out Shelton Road?"

"Just past Yadkin Road, maybe fifty yards past." He tapped his notes. "At least, that's what the chief told me."

"Can you drive us there?"

"Your mother told me you'd ask that, but no, I can't. The chief told me to stay here and watch over the town." He pointed at me. "Which is a good thing I did."

"Yes, sir, and thank you."

Charlie looked back at the map.

"He was on his way home and hit a tree." He looked back at Officer Nettles. "An accident?"

"Well, we don't know yet, Charlie. It looks that way."

I pointed out the window. "The patrol car is here, so was he in his personal car, his '53 Ford?"

"Yes."

"Is it still at the scene?"

"For now, yes. A wrecker is supposed to pick it up around nine and take it to the Ford dealer in Aberdeen. It will be im-pounded there."

I scanned Lewis's desk.

"Was there a journal, notepad, or something here that could tell us what he'd been doing, who he'd been interviewing, or something like that?"

"I didn't find anything, but I wasn't looking, so let me check." He opened and closed the drawers, then looked up. "Nothing here."

"Then he might have had something like that with him. If so, we need to get out there and find it before someone else does. Knowing who he's been dealing with on the Officer Lum murder, I'm not so sure it was an accident. With a wreck like that, someone who didn't know him might assume he'd hit that tree because he'd been drinking, but he didn't drink. Well, I saw him drink a glass of wine at Thanksgiving dinner, but that's it."

"I agree, but remember, the chief has already been at the scene. He would have collected and secured anything like that."

I looked at Charlie and then back to Officer Nettles.

"I wouldn't count on that."

I heard the front door open, footsteps, then, "Anybody home?"

Officer Nettles stood and yelled out the door.

"Be right there!"

He looked back at us.

"Be right back."

He walked into the main office, and I heard a deep voice say, "I'm Abe Bullard from Raleigh. Looking for Detective Lewis or Chief McDonald."

I stood and tiptoed to the wall by the doorway.

"Good to meet you, Bullard. I'm Tom Nettles from the Pinehurst PD. Been expecting you."

The raise-up panel in the counter squeaked.

"Understand this is your first day."

"Yeah, I was to get a little orientation, then pick up a uniform and go to work."

"Got your uniform and some paperwork for you in the office here."

I scurried back to my seat. When they entered, we stood. Officer Nettles introduced us to Officer Bullard, who wore a charcoal suit, white shirt, and blue tie. He was just as thick and husky as his voice, plus he had the dark hair and bushy eyebrows to go with it.

While Officer Nettles got the paperwork from the side drawer, he asked us to wait in the lobby.

Charlie went straight to the Coke machine. I went to the phone on Mom's desk and dialed the hospital number I found in her address book. The hospital operator paged her.

"Mrs. Hawke speaking."

"Mom, it's me."

"Where are you?"

"I'm with Charlie at the SPPD. We just found out about Detective Lewis."

"Are you okay?"

"Sure, Mom, I'm fine." I didn't think it was a good time to mention my little skirmish with Jasper Barnes.

"Did you have a good breakfast?"

"Oh, yes, ma'am. Great breakfast, plus we learned some

good stuff about the case. It's about Miss Tuley. But how's Detective Lewis?"

She sighed. "He's not good, Nate, not good: Lost a lot of blood, broken ribs, broken jaw, punctured lung. He's still in intensive care and still unconscious."

"Oh, man, I hate that, Mom. So, he hasn't said anything."

"No."

"Is the chief there?"

"He's here, but he's leaving soon; got to get back to the office and relieve Officer Nettles. Did Officer Bullard show up?"

"Yes, ma'am. Is he the 'you-know-who' guy?"

"That's him. I'll tell you more about him later. I want you to do your shopping or whatever else you have to do, then go home where I can reach you when I need you."

"Yes, ma'am, but shouldn't someone go secure the crash scene? I mean, it may look like an accident, but maybe it wasn't. If they would kill Officer Lum because he was on their tail, wouldn't they try to take out the guy who took over Lum's investigation?"

"Oh, I don't know, Nate. Let's not worry about that right now. Just shop and go home, okay?"

I crossed my fingers. "Yes, ma'am."

After I hung up, I turned to find Charlie in the heavy wooden chair in front of the front window and close to the Coke machine. He lifted a six-ounce Coke to me.

"What now, Kemosabe?"

"Shelton Road."

It took about fifteen minutes of pedaling before I saw a blue-and-white wrecker ahead on the right. It was parked by the side of the road just ahead of a large oak tree, with the front of a dark-red '53 Ford with a white top wrapped around it. As we approached, two men stepped out of the cab, so they must have just arrived. I turned to Charlie.

"Pick up the pace. I want to look in that car before they hook it up."

We stood on the pedals.

Along the last hundred yards to the scene, I noticed fresh car tracks in the damp soil barely off the edge of the road—two sets of tracks, both close together, and they did not belong to the wrecker. The inside tracks led to the tree—the only tree of any kind for a hundred yards—but did so in a wavy pattern, like that car had struggled to get back on the road.

We stopped on the right side of the wreck, which was only a few yards off the road, and dismounted. While the two guys unloaded some chains from the back of their truck, I stuck my head in the passenger window frame. The window lay shattered on the front seat and floorboard. I didn't see a journal, but I saw a blood-soaked and crushed steering wheel that turned my stomach. I took a couple of breaths, then tried the door. Stuck.

Charlie pulled open the backdoor.

"I'm in, Nate."

"See anything like a notepad or journal?"

"No, not yet."

I hustled around to the side where the driver's door had been pried open and left to hang by one hinge, but one of the guys with the wrecker saw me.

"Hey, kid, get away from there!"

I turned. "Yes, sir, I will in a minute. Detective Lewis left his notepad here, and my mother said Chief McDonald wanted me to get it for him. He can't leave the hospital right now. My mother works for the chief."

"Oh, okay. Well, look for it, then vamoose. We've got to drag this out of here, and we don't want you in our way."

"We understand, sir."

Charlie tapped me.

"Nate. Is this it?" He held up a black appointment book. "Found it under the front seat."

"Looks like it could be."

I held out my hand, and Charlie handed it to me over the seat back.

I flipped to the last page labeled December 21. It read: *0900 interview Mr. Buster Barnes in office, 1000 interview Miss Elsa Creech in Office, 1100 call Bullard, 1300 interview Mr. Ray Urdenbach in office, 1430 meet casket at mortuary, 1500 funeral at Manly Cemetery, 1600 interview Miss Jean Ann Tuley in office.*

Charlie tapped me again. "Well?"

"Well, this is his appointment book, so it tells me what he was up to, but it doesn't tell me the results."

"Maybe there's something else back here."

He disappeared behind the seat.

Someone hollered, "Hey!"

I turned. The tallest and skinniest of the two guys jangled toward us with chains draped over his shoulder and a cigarette hanging out of his mouth.

"Time's up, kids."

"Yes, sir, we're almost done."

"No, you *are* done. Now."

He dropped the chains behind the rear bumper.

Charlie backed out of the backdoor and looked at the skinny guy.

"Say, mister…How do you do this anyhow? What's the procedure? I've always wondered about that."

I saw blood-splattered keys in the ignition, grabbed them, then crawled over the glass to the glove compartment.

"Oh hell, we wrap the chains around the rear axle, back the wrecker up to it, then drag it away."

"But it's not going to roll away on those front tires. They're both flat as a pancake."

"Well, in this case, we'll have to drag it out far enough to get to the front. Then we'll back the wrecker up to it, hoist the front end up with that hooker in the bed of the truck, and—"

"Let the man do his job, Charlie."

I backed out the front door and wiped the blood from the keys and the glass cuts on my hands onto my jeans.

"Nate, you sure?"

I nodded and thumped the bulge under my windbreaker.

"I'm sure. Let's roll."

On the ride back to town, I turned to Charlie.

"Those tire tracks leading to the tree tell me someone ran him off the road. We need a camera; we need to take pictures of those tracks."

Charlie flipped his hair out of his eyes.

"And that tree was the only tree around, like whoever ran him off the road knew it was there and drove him into it."

"Exactly."

"This was a 'hit' job, Nate."

"Yep."

We rode straight to downtown and the SPPD. In the parking lot, we caught Officer Nettles just as he opened the door to his Pinehurst patrol car, a black-and-white Ford. We stopped beside him.

I straddled my bike with my tennis shoes on the asphalt and looked up at him.

"Officer Nettles, are you leaving?"

"Yeah, Nate. Gotta get back to Pinehurst. Officer Bullard can take over here. He's an experienced officer from Raleigh."

"But he can't leave town, right?"

"Not 'til the chief gets back, no."

"We need someone with a camera to go to the crash site and take some pictures of tire tracks. And do it quick before the wrecker or gawkers mess them up. Can you help us?"

He crossed his arms.

"Oh, I don't know, Nate. They're expecting me back this morning. Besides, wouldn't Chief McDonald have done that?"

"The chief never carries a camera." I didn't know that for a fact, but...

He looked at his watch.

I looked at mine.

"It's still early, sir, and it's only five minutes away."

"Okay, well, that would give me time to do it, but I don't have a camera."

"Detective Lewis has a camera, and I'll bet it's in the locker in his office."

He grinned. "If it is, I'll do it."

It was, and he did.

We were back at the SPPD in twenty minutes. Officer Nettles took the photos to the drugstore to be developed, and Charlie and I walked down to the hardware store to finish our shopping. After all, I'd promised Mom I'd "Go shopping and go home," so that was what I intended to do. She didn't say I couldn't go anywhere else before I went shopping.

As we rolled our bikes into the bike stand in front of the hardware store, Jimmy Rayburn came out the door with his mother. At least, I assumed it was his mother. She looked older than my mom but had the same blonde hair, blue eyes, and pale complexion as Jimmy.

When he paused beside us, she said, "Come on, Jimmy."

"Mom, this is, this is Nate Hawke and Charlie Shonkasabe—the two boys who beat up that man this morning. Remember what that lady inside told us?"

She stopped and eyed us.

"Really? You two?"

Charlie stepped up.

"No, ma'am, you know how rumors can get started. We didn't beat up anybody, let alone a grown man."

She huffed. "Well, I didn't think so."

She motioned to Jimmy. "Come on."

"Mom, I wanna, I wanna talk with these guys a minute. They're in my class at school. Can't I meet you at Pace's?"

She looked down the crowded sidewalk at Pace's Department Store. Adults and children with shopping bags poured in and out through their double doors. She looked back at Jimmy.

"Five minutes, Jimmy. I'll be in men's clothing." She turned and wove herself and her shopping bag down the sidewalk between hurried people.

I said, "What's up, Jimmy?"

"Hey…" He looked at Charlie, then at me. "Are, are you guys going to that Girl Scout dance tonight?"

Charlie propped his arm on Jimmy's shoulder.

"We'll be there, Jimmy, and we'll help you break the ice with little Miss Molly if you like."

"Oh, well, I wasn't worried about that." He rubbed his head through his short hair. "I was just wondering if you guys would wear a coat and tie."

I grinned. "Are you kidding? My mom wouldn't let me out of the house without a coat and tie. In her mind, this is a big deal."

"Same here, Jimmy. Wear your best Sunday-go-to-meetin' outfit, and you'll be good." Charlie leaned into him. "But leave your spurs at home. Girls don't dig spurs."

"I don't, I don't have spu—" Billy looked over my shoulder. His eyes widened.

"Quick, Nate. Turn around. See that short, skinny man in the plaid shirt and jeans heading for the door?"

I turned. "Yeah?"

"Mr. Alderson."

"Dark complexion, unshaven?"

"That's him."

Charlie scoffed. "He doesn't look that threatening, Jimmy."

Alderson fell in behind another man in jeans and entered the store.

"He doesn't look it, but he must be plenty tough. I mean, I mean, he works under cars all day. I think he's the muffler guy at Aberdeen Ford."

I grinned. "He's got the build for slithering under cars."

Jimmy looked down the street, then stepped backward toward Pace's.

"I gotta go, guys. See you tonight."

I raised my hand. "In a coat and tie?"

"Yeah, yeah, sure."

We entered the hardware store and were immediately emersed in the noise of jostling people clambering around one another and talking over the noise and the jolly Christmas music. We pressed on. Halfway down the crowded aisle, we ran into Chipper. She stood by a display of dog collars and leashes and dropped a rhinestone collar into her shopping bag.

I tapped her on the shoulder. "Shopping for Sofie?"

She turned just as Charlie stepped up.

"Well, she's not shopping for you, Nate. You don't wear rhinestones."

"You two! I've been hearing about you guys. Got Mr. Barnes arrested, huh?" She pointed at me. "I heard he chased you around the store; you fought him off, then Charlie put him away with a hammer!"

She looked at Charlie.

"Did you crack his skull? Was he bleeding?"

"No, no crack, no bleed. I hit him with a rubber mallet."

"Well, I guess you know that puts you two on his you-know-what list."

"Yeah, I guess it does, but it seemed like the only thing to do at the time." He nodded at me. "I couldn't let my Kemosabe be dragged off."

She leaned in and whispered, "Hey, any news on the case?"

I glanced at Charlie. "Yeah, lots, but maybe we shouldn't talk about it here."

She nodded. "I've got news too. Tell you about it tonight, okay?

"Deal."

She worked her way to the front cashier, and Charlie and I split up. I got the Milk-Bone biscuits and beef jerky for Superman, and he got a new rubber mallet for his father to use with his furniture-building hobby. We pedaled home, our gifts secure in paper sacks in my basket.

Along the way, we talked about the party and what they might have to eat, then we talked about the basketball game Friday night. I didn't think Mom would want to leave Detective Lewis and drive us, so Charlie said his dad would do it. He was a basketball fan from North Carolina State and rarely missed a Southern Pines game.

After that, we hardly said a word. Charlie was probably planning how he would ace me out of dancing with Chipper, but I was still on the case. I looked forward to the dance and hearing what Chipper had to say, but in my mind, and based on what I'd seen at the crime scene plus what I'd learned at Benny's, I only needed one more piece of evidence to move Miss Tuley to the head of the class. I pressed my fist against the front of my windbreaker and felt the journal and appointment book against my stomach. That piece would undoubtedly be in the journal.

Chapter 11

XX AND THE STING

After I got home from the hardware store, I opened Superman's gate, and he bounded toward the back fence. At first, I thought he would get the tennis ball we couldn't find that morning and bring it to me, but that thought vanished when a tabby cat jumped the wire fence. It disappeared into the woods behind us. Superman slid to a stop at the fence, then looked back at me with a drooped head and squinted eyes like *Rats! I thought I had him that time!*

While he sulked, I poured some fresh water for him. Overhead the thick, dark clouds pressed even lower and moved even faster. I hadn't heard a weather report, but it looked like rain, which meant the tire tracks at the crash scene would be erased—not good if those pictures Officer Nettles took did not come out clear and crisp.

I stepped over to the basket on my bike and opened the paper sack that contained Superman's Christmas presents. I retrieved Lewis's appointment book and the journal from inside my shirt and put them in the sack, but then immediately pulled the journal out. No one had ever accused me of being good at delayed gratification. I flipped to the last page.

The backdoor squeaked.

"Nate."

I stuffed the journal back into the sack and looked over to see Becky, in Mom's green dress, leaning out the doorway.

"Mom's on the phone and wants to speak with you." She snickered. "Hope you have a good excuse for being late."

"I'm not late. She didn't give me a time to be home."

"Maybe not, but she thinks you're late and her perception, my dear brother, is all that matters."

"'Perception,' huh? Big word."

"It's a good word. We had it in class last week, plus Gill uses it. He makes straight A's, you know; really smart." She looked up at the swollen clouds. "He's just dreamy."

"Yeah, well, dream on, big sister."

I glanced over at Superman sniffing around a fence post. "Meanwhile, unless you want to put Superman away for me, tell Mom I'll take care of that and be right there."

"Okay."

She took a half step back, leaned out the doorway again, and cocked her head.

"Hey. What happened to your cheek?"

I touched my right cheek where Mr. Barnes had hit me.

"What do you mean?"

"Is that a bruise?"

She stepped out and walked toward me with squinted eyes.

"Well...looks like it's not a full bruise yet, but it's red and headed that way."

She stopped in front of me and reached out to touch my cheek.

I blocked her hand. "It's nothing. Don't worry about it."

"Yeah, it is something." She stuck her hands to her hips.

"Okay, little brother, who did this, and who do I have to kill to defend the family name? Tom Ray?"

I scoffed. "Just forget about it, okay? I got hit by a door."

"'Hit by a door,' my foot. Come on, give."

"No give. Just leave me alone and let me put Superman away so I can talk with Mom."

"Okay, Mr. Secretive, but I'm not buyin' your story." She dropped her hands and turned for the backdoor. "I'll get it out of you later. Meanwhile, I'll tell Mom you're on your way."

"Thanks, and don't mention the door accident."

"Ha! She's Mom; she needs to know."

"Wait! Is she still at the hospital?"

"No. Office."

A minute later, I picked up the phone and heard the disconnect tone.

I walked to my room and stashed the sack with the appointment book and journal in the bottom drawer of the dresser I shared with Granddaddy. I returned to the kitchen and dialed the number for the SPPD.

"Southern Pines Police, Mrs. Hawke."

"Hi, Mom, it's me. Sorry I didn't get to the phone sooner."

"Hold on a minute, Nate."

I heard her loosely cup the phone, but in the background, I could still hear men's voices. One voice was very loud and angry, the other calm, but I couldn't understand what they were saying. The back and forth went on for a minute, and then I heard a door slam. Mom's hand slid off the speaker.

"Nate, you still there?"

"Yes, ma'am. What's going on?"

"Oh, just routine stuff. It's you I want to talk about. Are you okay?"

"Yes, ma'am, I'm fine. How's Detective Lewis?"

"Still in intensive care, but at least his vital signs are stronger. The doctors were more optimistic when I left because he had minimal brain swelling, and it had already gone down."

"Still unconscious?"

"Yes, unfortunately. But Nate, Officer Bullard says Mr. Barnes hit you and tried to kidnap you."

"Well, he did, sort of, but it wasn't much; I'm okay. Is Mr. Barnes still there?"

"No, that was him leaving. The judge in Aberdeen said we had to let him go until we had a hearing."

"A hearing? Like to decide if there will be a trial?"

"That's correct, Counselor Nate, but that won't be until after Christmas."

"Oh."

"Meanwhile, you stay away from him, understand?"

"Oh, I will, Mom, no problem. Did Officer Bullard tell you about the crash scene?"

"Yes, and Officer Nettles left me a note about the pictures he took. When I called the drugstore, they said the pictures would be ready tomorrow."

"Not sooner?"

"No, the developer guy is the druggist, Doc Phillburn, who was out doing his Christmas shopping."

"Oh, okay. Someone intentionally ran Detective Lewis off the road, Mom. I'm sure of it."

"How do you know?"

"Oh…well, Officer Nettles described the scene to me."

"If that's true, then we're dealing with attempted homicide."

"Yes, ma'am. I think that's exactly what we're dealing with."

"Then that's another reason you should stay out of this, Nate. No more encounters with Jasper Barnes or anyone else you might suspect. You understand me?"

"Yes, ma'am. No more encounters."

"That's right." She paused. "How's your face?"

"My face? Well, everyone still says I look like Dad in your wedding photograph."

She chuckled. "Nice try. Your face today, Nathan Hawke—where Mr. Barnes hit you."

"It's okay, Mom. A little red, no blood."

"Did Officer Nettles take a picture of your face?"

"No, ma'am."

"Well, come on down here, and let's do that. For evidence."

Ah, crap, not now. The journal!

"Can't it wait 'til later, Mom? Say four o'clock?"

"Why? What are you up to?"

"I've ah…I've got to fix lunch, then ah…wrap Christmas presents—you know, while you aren't here and Granddaddy is still in his workshop. Are the wrapping paper and ribbon still in the hall closet?"

"As long as that's all you're going to do, then yes, four o'clock, and yes, they're in the hall closet. But if I call this afternoon, you better be there wrapping gifts, young man."

"I'll be here, Mom. I promise." *I may be reading a journal, but I'll be here.*

As soon as I hung up the phone, Granddaddy wheezed in through the backdoor. After a coughing spasm, he headed for the bathroom.

"Granddaddy…you need the humidifier?"

From the dining room, I heard, "Yes, please! Be right back!"

I got Granddaddy's humidifier up to steam.

When he returned, he hung a white towel over his head and leaned over the humidifier to soak up the lung-comforting mist. I opened a can of Campbell's tomato soup and laid out the hamburger meat for Granddaddy's famous "Gut Bomb Burgers" (heavy on the jalapeños).

When we sat down at the kitchen table with the soup and saltines and waited for the hamburgers to bake, Granddaddy cleared his throat.

"Did you know Lum was going to sell his car?"

I let my next spoon full of soup slide back into the bowl.

"No, sir, no one has mentioned that. How do you know?"

"I saw it in the classifieds this morning in last week's *Pilot*. I brought the paper home from the hospital last Friday but didn't get around to reading the whole thing until this morning. He wanted three hundred dollars for it: A 1953 Ford coupe with white walls, straight-six, and three on the tree. In other words, a standard, three-speed transmission with the shifter on the steering wheel column. Blue."

"Yes, sir. I've seen it at the SPPD. He kept it clean too, but we haven't seen it since last Friday, the day Detective Lewis thinks he was killed."

"Then they're looking for a murderer *and* a car thief?"

I finished my last scoop of soup.

"And a robber. His body was picked clean."

The oven timer buzzed, so I got up and retrieved the hamburgers with the crispy jalapeños on top. The lettuce, salsa, and shredded mozzarella cheese were already on the table.

After lunch, Granddaddy went back to his workshop. Becky had gone to have lunch with Jenny, then they were going shopping, so the house was quiet for a change. I walked to my room and retrieved the appointment book and journal from the dresser.

Seated at my maple desk in front of the window on the far side of our bedroom, I took another look at the light-blue journal and realized it was Lum's journal, the one I'd seen in the trunk of our car. *Maybe Lewis didn't keep a journal.*

I flipped to the last page and read Lum's last entry: *Friday: Pick up Jean Ann at 1100. XX will have more for me after the game—park.*

XX? Code for someone?

I heard the phone ring. I slipped the journal into my desk drawer and hustled to the kitchen.

"Hawke's residence, Nate speaking."

"Nate, did you go to that wreck scene?"

Crap. There was a definite bite to Mom's tone, so once

again, the promise I'd made to Mom back in October was cramping my style.

"Ah…yes, ma'am. Charlie and I did. Just briefly."

"I just talked with the wrecker guys, and they told me you were there, but they didn't see you leave with anything…anything like a journal, maybe?"

"A journal?"

"A journal, Nate—Gunner's journal. The same journal he left in my car when I took him to pick up his car Friday morning after it was serviced. The same journal you tried to get out of my trunk early yesterday morning. Did you or did you not find it at the scene of the wreck?"

"Are you sure the wrecker guys didn't get it?"

"Nathan! One more time…Did you or did you not find that journal?"

I hung my head. *Busted.*

"Yes, ma'am, I have it."

"Get it down here—now! You've got five minutes!"

"Yes, ma'am. On my way."

Okay, I had to give up the journal, but I still had Lewis's appointment book. That was something, but I really needed to see Lewis's notes from his interviews with Buster Barnes, Ray Urdenbach, and Lum's girlfriends. Charlie and I didn't see anything else at the scene of the wreck, so if he had a journal, or if he kept notes on his interviews—which he most certainly would have done—they would be in his office.

Outside, in my windbreaker and ball cap, I mounted my bike and rolled down our driveway. At the same time, I scanned the last page of the journal, which was very interesting reading. "The plot thickened," as Chipper would say. I tossed the journal into my basket and picked up the pace.

After dodging some heavy downtown traffic, I dismounted at the SPPD, slipped my bike into the bike rack, wove between a few shoppers, then jogged up the walkway toward the door.

Mom opened the door just as I got there. She frowned and held out her hand.

I handed over the journal and took a deep breath.

"Mom...I only did what Chief McDonald should have done in the first place. Don't I at least get a thank-you?"

The frown melted away. She shook her head and smiled.

"Yes, darlin,' of course." She held out her arms to me. "Thank you, and thank you for telling me the truth."

We hugged, and I said, "Any news on Detective Lewis?"

"No, no change yet."

"Well, I didn't see any patrol cars in the parking lot. What's going on? Is anyone looking for Officer Lum's murderer? Is anyone looking for the guy who ran Detective Lewis into that tree? Is anybody doing anything?"

She put her arm around me.

"Come on inside and sit down, Nate. You sound as frustrated and as concerned as I am." She held the door for me. "Let's talk about it."

Inside, I sat at the duty officer's desk.

Mom sat at her desk, slipped Officer Lum's journal into the top drawer, then rolled her chair closer to me.

"The chief is at a meeting of Moore County officers in Aberdeen. Officer Bullard is on patrol, so to answer your question, no one is doing anything right now. Unless the chief is discussing these things with the county sheriff in Aberdeen."

"What are the odds of that?"

"Probably slim to none."

"Then it's just us, Mom. We care, we're concerned, so why don't we do something?"

"I'd like to, but I can't leave the office; I can't leave the phone." She pointed at me. "And I certainly don't want you out there looking for murderers. That brush you had with Mr. Barnes scared me, Nate. Enough of that."

"I don't think we'll need to leave. I think the answers are right here in this office—they're in Officer Lum's journal and Detective Lewis's notes, which are probably in his office."

Her eyes narrowed. "How much of Gunner's journal did you read?"

"Enough to know something was going down, some kind of operation was in motion, and it involved *XX,* whoever that is."

She looked away, that thoughtful look, like she was trying to make a decision, then she rolled back to her desk and took Lum's journal from the drawer.

"Okay, I'll tell you what I know, which isn't much, then we'll go through this journal and see what we can come up with. As for Dan's notes, he didn't keep a journal that I know of. He made pencil notes, and then he would ask me to type them. They're in a file in his office."

Finally!

She opened the journal and flipped back a few pages from the last entry.

"Gunner was doing the legwork for Dan on the bike thefts, the car thefts, and of course, dealing with Mr. Alderson and his pile of tickets. The bootlegging situation we had put on the back burner until we could stop the other crimes."

She put her finger on an entry in the journal.

"On Monday, December twelfth, Gunner, Dan, and Officer Bullard met in Raleigh to discuss a sting operation."

She looked up.

"Officer Bullard was on the Raleigh police force then, but Dan was recruiting him for SPPD. Last Thursday, the day before Gunner was killed, Abe called us and said he'd resigned from the Raleigh PD and was coming to join us this week."

She looked back at the journal.

"That day, the twelfth, he writes, *My car will be the bait. Not crazy about that idea, but they say I'll be compensated if it's damaged.*"

She looked up again.

"He was to put an ad in the paper that would tell a potential thief how the car was equipped and what it looked like. If the thieves needed a car like that, they would show up. They felt sure someone here in this area—probably someone right here in Southern Pines—was a contact for the thieves. Gunner was officially on vacation, but he was really going to meet potential buyers during the day and be upstairs in his apartment watching his car at night."

"So, who is XX? And how does that fit in?"

"I can't tell you yet, but if we find it in his journal, then you read it, then I didn't tell you."

She looked back at the journal and flipped through a few more pages.

"He doesn't put a name to XX, but he mentions XX, oh, maybe four times in that time period." She took another look. "But it appears he only met with XX in person on two occasions, and…that last entry referred to what would have been their third meeting. 'Park' must mean the city park behind the SPPD."

"And *after the game*, would that be after the basketball game last week?"

"Probably. Gunner never missed a Southern Pines basketball game."

"Has anyone met with *XX* since? Has anyone resumed working the case and the sting operation?"

"Now that Gunner and his car are gone, that sting operation is history." She gazed at the floor. "Sad history, I'm afraid. Very sad. I really miss that little guy."

She pointed at a medicine-like tube on the top of the duty desk where I sat.

"That's his tube of liniment. Poor guy was sore all over from his karate classes with Miss Tuley." She nodded to the restroom door in the corner and chuckled.

"He'd go in there and rub liniment on his shoulders and neck, and then he'd come back in here smelling like a pro football locker room and say, 'I'm Korean! I should be better at that karate stuff!'" She smiled. "Funny guy."

"I liked him too. He was always good to me, but Mom… someone needs to meet up with XX. They—XX, I mean— could be the key to his murder."

"Yes, could be. Hey, speaking of keys…"

She took a key from her top drawer.

"If the answers aren't in Gunner's journal, then you're right. Let's go check Dan's desk."

I followed her into Lewis's office, where Mom plopped onto his roller chair and scooted up to his desk. She unlocked the file drawer on the bottom right side of the desk and then flipped through the files. She looked up.

"It's not here—a red manila file, red for hot." She pointed at his locker. "Try—no, it's padlocked."

"Oh yeah, but it wasn't locked earlier when Office Nettles got his camera."

"He must have locked it when he put the camera back." She scooted backward and hopped up. "Be right back. I think I remember it, but just to be sure…"

"Remember what?"

"His birthday!"

"His birthday?"

"For the combination!"

She reappeared in the doorway with a smile.

"May twenty-sixth, 1923." She stopped at the locker and grabbed the lock.

"Right to five…left to twenty-six…right to twenty-three." She pulled it down. Nothing. She jiggled it.

"Well, durn, Nate. I thought sure that would be it."

"I don't think it's one of those padlocks you can set, Mom. It looks like the kind they issue at school and comes with a preset combination." I looked at his desk.

"He must have that written down somewhere. Mind if I look?"

From the office, the radio crackled, and Chief McDonald's raspy voice said, "Chief to base."

Mom let the padlock fall against the locker and hurried into the office. She said over her shoulder, "Go ahead…and good luck!"

A second later, I heard, "Go ahead, Chief."

While I opened the top drawer in the center of the desk, I heard, "I'm inbound from Aberdeen. ETA in…ten. Anything hot?"

"Nothing hot right now, Chief. Officer Bullard is on patrol. No change in Dan's condition. Jasper Barnes was arrested for assault and attempted kidnapping, but he's been released pending a hearing."

"What? Who was arrested? Please tell me you didn't say, Jasper Barnes."

"Affirmative—Jasper Barnes."

"Who arrested him?"

"Officer Nettles. He was on duty when the assault call came in."

"Oh, for cryin' out loud. As if I don't have—Never mind. If there's nothin' hot, I'm goin' home. See you in the morning. Out."

"Copy that. Base out."

While that conversation had gone on, I hadn't moved. It had finally occurred to me that Lewis wouldn't have left his locker unlocked if the files had been in there, and Nettles must have locked it after he put the camera back.

Mom reappeared in the doorway. She put her hands on her hips.

"You know, Nate...you were right again. From now on, this is *our* case."

Chapter 12

THE BLUE PAINT CLUE

Finally, we were working the case together. Mom stepped up to Lewis's desk while I pulled out the top drawer and dumped the contents on the top of the desk.

She put her hands on her hips again.

"What are you doing?"

"I don't think we're going to find the files in his locker, but—" I turned the drawer onto its side and pointed to a yellow tag taped to the bottom.

"There's the combination. I saw this in a movie one time—a Sam Spade movie, I think." I turned the drawer sideways so I could read the tag. "You ready?"

"Ready." She stepped to the locker and grabbed the lock.

I read out the combination. It worked, but…no file.

Mom took the camera out of the locker, closed the locker door, then checked her watch.

"In one hour and three minutes, we're going to Dan's house. Mrs. Mannerly will let us in." She looked at me and cocked her head.

"Which gives me time to take that picture of your bruise."

I found a fresh roll of film in the pile of pens, paperclips, staples, rulers, notepads, and erasers on the desk. I handed it to her and scraped the rest of the pile into the drawer. After a couple of mug shots, I stepped to the door.

"Maybe I better get home before the rain comes."

She glanced out the window.

"Good idea. I'll pick you up at five-oh-five."

Outside, I snugged my cap down and walked toward my bike, but it occurred to me that while I was downtown, I might get lucky at the drugstore. Weaving between cars and trucks, I crossed Broad Street and the railroad tracks.

Inside the corner drugstore, gray-haired Doc Phillburn stood behind the dispensing counter in his white lab shirt with the buttons along the shoulder and neck. He didn't look up. An older couple sat at the table by the front window, and, to my disappointment, Becky sat with her buddy, Jenny, at the far corner table. The girls gabbed away between pulls on what looked like chocolate milkshakes. Neither seemed to notice me, which was a good thing and seeing Doc behind the counter was a very good thing.

I slipped onto a stool at the drink counter, a couple of stools up from two women in soft wool hats and coats, and kept my back to Becky. A heavyset teenage boy I'd seen at school but never met stood at the sink and spoke in a loud voice that made me cringe.

"What can I do for you, kid?"

From the corner, I heard giggles and then Jenny's high-pitched voice.

"Hey, Becky, there's Nate!"

I focused on the teenager.

"Ah…Mrs. Hawke sent me from the SPPD to pick up the photos Officer Nettles left here this morning."

He turned his head. "Doc. Photo's ready for SPPD yet?"

The doc kept his head down like he was busy counting pills. We waited. He finally looked up.

"Five o'clock. Should be ready by then."

From the corner, I heard, "Nate. Come here a minute."

I turned, and Becky waved to me.

"Over here, Joe Palooka." They giggled.

I gave her a dismissive wave and turned for the door.

A chair scraped on the linoleum floor.

"Seriously, Nate! Come here. Got some news."

I turned to see Becky walking toward me.

"Not now, Becky. I've got to get home before it rains. Tell me later."

She stopped in front of me, crossed her arms, and whispered, "So, you don't want to hear what Jenny knows about Officer Lum's murder?"

"How could Jenny know anything?"

"She lives next door to the house Officer Lum lived in, that's how."

"Oh."

I joined them at their table and sat in one of those wrought-iron chairs with the padded red-vinyl seats and heart-shaped back. Those chairs were never comfortable for me. I often wondered if they made them uncomfortable on purpose, so people would finish their sandwich or drink and leave.

I nodded to Jenny, who wore a pink dress and saddle oxfords. I called her Skinny Jenny, but not to her face—that would have been rude.

"Okay, Jenny. Whatcha got for me?"

She giggled and looked at Becky.

"He really does have a bruise—a big one."

"Jenny. I'm over here, and I'm in a hurry. What do you know about the murder?"

"Oh, well, I don't know anything about the murder, Nate. I didn't see it. All I know is Officer Lum stayed after the basketball game last Friday night, and I thought that was strange."

"What do you mean, 'He stayed?'"

"He just stayed in the stands. Well, he moved down to the front row, but Mom and Dad and I left for the exit with everyone else, and he stayed."

"Was he sitting with anyone?"

"No, I don't think so."

"That's all you've got? He stayed after the game?"

"Well, I did see him go by the house later."

She glanced at Becky and then back to me.

"Yeah, and that was kinda funny because he drove by his house and just kept going."

"Was he alone?"

"Uh-huh. But now that I think about it, the driver was bigger than Office Lum, so maybe it wasn't him. Maybe someone had borrowed his car."

"You're sure it was his car."

"Oh, for sure—nice ocean blue, white walls, and a longer-than-normal radio antenna. Yeah, it was his car."

"Anything else about the driver? Male or female, tall or short, big or small, hat or no hat?"

She looked down and stirred the straw in her milkshake.

"Male, no hat."

She stirred the drink again and then looked up.

"Yeah, male, no hat, and just bigger. That's all I could tell."

"Was he in a hurry?"

"Oh yeah, he drove by fast, not like Officer Lum at all. Officer Lum would always coast by, you know? So he could wave to us if we were out."

"And the time? Did you notice the time?"

"Didn't notice, but probably around ten fifteen. We always get home from the game at ten, but last Friday, I left my purse in the car, so I had to go back out to the car and get it. That's when I saw him go by; about ten fifteen, maybe ten twenty."

"And you live on South May, right?"

"Uh-huh. A block before Morganton Road."

"Did you see him get to Morganton and notice which way he turned?"

"He turned right."

Toward the tree farm!

I slid my chair back and stood.

"Thanks, Jenny. Good information."

I dug out a quarter from my jeans and plopped it on the table.

"Have another milkshake on me."

Becky slapped the table.

"Hey, how about me? I'm the one that told you about her!"

"Just your luck—I'm out of quarters."

"I'll share mine with you, Becky." Then as I walked away, Jenny added, "He's really cute, you know?"

"Yeah, cute like a butt boil."

Outside, scattered raindrops splattered against the sidewalk and drove the shopping crowd indoors. I jogged back across the street, the tracks, and the traffic to get to the SPPD.

When I got to the bike rack, my windbreaker and cap were wet but not soaked. I pulled my bike out of the rack and rolled it into the SPPD lobby with me. Mom had the phone to her ear and motioned me to sit at the duty desk.

She nodded. "I know the address, ma'am, and I'll get Officer Bullard over there right away…Yes, ma'am…Bullard, that's right. He's new…Goodbye."

She looked at me.

"Phew, that woman can talk, but I feel for her living next door to the Aldersons and their constant fights."

She rolled her chair over to the radio on the table behind her.

"Be right with you, Nate."

She flipped up the transmit switch and picked up the mic. "Base to patrol."

"Go ahead, base."

"Got a ten-sixteen at four-one-eight Ridley Street. See the lady at four-one-four. Be advised, we've been there many times before."

"Ten-four. ETA in five."

"Copy. Base out."

She flipped the switch and looked at me.

"I thought you went home."

I sat in the roller chair at the duty desk.

"Thought I'd see about the pictures first, and good news—they'll be ready at five."

I checked the clock on the wall.

"Ten more minutes. Plus, I've got some news on the Lum case."

"Well, spill it, Sherlock."

"First, he was seen at the basketball game, and he remained behind in the stands after the game was over, even while everyone else was leaving. Later, his car, driven by a man bigger than him, was seen on South May Street turning right onto Morganton Road at around ten fifteen to ten twenty last Friday night."

"Humm. From the school gym, that's the way to Barnes's farm."

"Yes, ma'am. So, I'm thinking the driver was the murderer, and the body was in the trunk." I scooted closer. "Could the murderer be XX?"

"Oh, no, I don't think so." She pushed some loose hair back into her bun.

"You know, Mom, the driver could have been the murderer, but he also could have been an accomplice. Either way, it seems to narrow down the time of death."

She tapped a pencil eraser on her desk.

"How big was the driver?"

"My informant didn't know. Just bigger than Officer Lum."

"Your informant, huh?" She grinned. "You don't want to ID your informant, Mr. Hawke?"

"Okay, it was Jenny. When I went over to check on the

photos, she and Becky were in the drugstore sucking down a milkshake."

"Oh, of course. Jenny lives next door to the house where Gunner rented that upstairs apartment."

"Yes, ma'am." I cocked my head. "Mom, if Officer Lum was dating Miss Tuley, and they had been shopping for a Christmas tree that afternoon, why wasn't she with him at the basketball game?"

"She teaches one of her women's self-defense classes on Friday night, so she was probably in Fayetteville."

"Okay, but what time does that class end?"

"I don't know, but if you're thinking she had time to teach her class then get over here and commit a murder, I'm sure that was possible. But why would you suspect her?"

I raised my eyebrows.

"We're on this case together now, right, Mom? No secrets—even though you still won't tell me who XX is. I mean, think about it: If you're waiting on permission from Detective Lewis to tell me, that could take a while."

"Okay, I'll tell you. Geez. But first, tell me why you suspect that sweet Miss Tuley."

"We have a deal?"

"Yes, deal; now why do you suspect Miss Tuley?"

I cleared my throat.

"When I found the body wrapped in that army blanket, two fingers were sticking out of the top of it. Those two fingers, the pointer finger and the middle finger stuck out from his curled hand like he was signaling the number *two*, as in Tuley. That's why I suspect her, but I don't have a motive. Now, you told me one time that Detective Lewis had gone to Fayetteville to check her out. Did he tell you what he found or if he found anything?"

"Two fingers for Tuley, huh? Well, I guess that's possible. No, Dan didn't tell me anything, but if he'd made notes about what he'd learned, those notes would have been in his file or still in his notebook. I haven't seen that notebook or typed anything for him since the funeral. Another reason why we need to get to his house and look for those things."

"And soon, but wouldn't it have been with him in his car?"

"Not if he had gone home after work, then gone out again."

She looked up at the clock on the wall between the two offices.

"Okay, it's five o'clock. Why don't you run back over—" A sheet of rain pounded against the windows. "Oops, maybe not." She smiled. "Well, I guess we're stuck here for a while. Unless you want to join me under my umbrella and let me drive you to the drugstore."

I stood and pointed at the umbrella in the corner behind the counter.

"If you let me borrow your umbrella, I'll run to the drugstore now, probably faster than driving. But first...Who is XX?"

"Okay, but go. The traffic will be awful in a minute. I'll tell you about XX when you get back. Meanwhile, I'm going back into Dan's office and have another look at his files. I still think the Barneses or the Heisters have something to do with Gunner's murder, Dan's wreck, or both."

I grabbed the umbrella and flipped up the panel on the counter.

"I still think it's Miss Tuley." I stopped at the door. "Maybe she has a bad temper, maybe he jilted her Friday, and she strangled him."

"Ha! Maybe I'll strangle you if you don't get to the drugstore."

I opened the door to a gust of wind, a spray of rain, and winter's darkness. I held down the bill of my cap and turned.

"You strangle me, and I'll report you for child abuse—if I live. Bye!"

When I returned to the SPPD, my jeans and tennis shoes were soaked, but I had the photos. I plopped back onto the roller chair at the duty desk and scooted over to Mom's desk. We examined the photos together.

The tire tracks clearly showed he'd been intentionally forced off the road and run into that oak tree. The skid marks at the end also showed that, in the dark, he'd seen the tree at the last minute but too late to avoid it. Mom agreed and called Chief McDonald.

After she explained the evidence in the photos to him, she said, "Did you see any files or notebooks in the car or at the scene?"

I heard him scream, "Hell, no. I told you that at the hospital!"

I leaned closer to the earpiece.

Mom stayed with her calm, talk-with-a-child voice.

"Did you see any signs of another car at the scene, like someone had stopped and searched the car?"

"No, Mrs. Hawke, I did not. Now, I'm tired, and it's almost supper time, so tell Bullard he's on duty tonight, and I'll see you both in the morning."

I backed off.

Mom hung up and looked at me.

"Well, he might not have seen any signs of another car—probably didn't even look—but I see signs there was another car, and they stopped."

She pointed to the upper part of the last photo.

"Look at these tracks: a one-eighty. Someone came to the scene from the opposite direction, stopped, did a one-eighty, and took off. And they had new or almost new tires."

She took another look at the other photos.

"I can't tell if it was the same car that ran him off the road, but the tire marks look the same."

"Mom, two questions: What if the person in the car that did the one-eighty stopped and got Detective Lewis's notes or file from the wreck? Also, do you see any scrape marks on Detective Lewis's car, maybe paint from the car that ran him off the road?"

"I'll tackle the paint question first."

She flipped through a few more photos until she found one of the left side of the car.

"I'll tell you one thing, Nate: Officer Nettles is good. He knew exactly what to photograph."

She pointed at the left front fender just above the dented wheel well.

"Blue paint."

"That would rule out Jasper Barnes unless he was driving

something other than his rusty red pickup. What color car does Miss Tuley drive?"

She pursed her lips. "Blue. Gunner showed me a picture of them in front of it. Her roommate in Fayetteville took it a couple of weeks ago."

She nodded at the duty desk.

"Check the top drawer. Maybe it's there."

I opened the drawer, and the two smiled back at me. "Bin-go."

I picked it up, closed the drawer, and showed it to Mom.

"There's your killer and her *blue* Plymouth."

Mom scoffed, "Come on, Nate. That sweet young thing? Look at that smile." She flipped the picture. "That's a loving smile, not the smile of a killer."

"I'll bet Delilah smiled lovingly at Sampson too."

"Well...I still can't imagine it was Miss Tuley. Call it woman's intuition."

"Okay, who else on our list of suspects drives a blue car or truck?"

"In the Barnes family, there's Buster, the father, and Junior. I've seen Junior in a red Buick—he's been more financially successful than Jasper—but I don't know what Buster drives." Her eyes brightened.

"I've got an idea. I want to check on Dan before we go home, so we'll go by the Barneses' on the way to the hospital. We can take a look then. How 'bout that?"

"Good plan, but first...Can you tell from those photos if anyone got out of the one-eighty car?"

She took another look. "No, afraid not."

"Well, rats…but it's still Miss Tuley. Once she saw him slumped over the steering wheel, she wouldn't have wanted to get out of the car and take his pulse. Too messy."

She reached over and patted my shoulder.

"If you insist."

"I do insist, and I also insist that you finally tell me who Mr. XX is. Please?"

"Ah, Mr. XX. Well, Mr. XX is actually Miss XX, as in Rachel Turner."

"Rachel Turner! He was dating her, *and* she was helping with the sting?"

"No, Nate, he wasn't dating her at all. She was too young even for Gunner." She held up her hand. "Hold on—gotta get back to work."

She rolled over to the radio, told Officer Bullard he was on duty that night, then signed off. She rolled back to her desk. She called home, told Becky we were leaving and asked her to start supper. She nodded to me.

"Quittin' time, Nate. Let's launch."

She pulled her purse and coat out of a bottom drawer, then walked to the front door and locked it. She walked back through the opening on the counter.

"Let's go see Dan."

I stood. "But Mom…Rachel? The sting?"

I joined her as she walked toward the backdoor.

"Okay. Rachel had met Gunner months ago when he helped her and her mother with a flat tire out on Highway One. Then, a couple of weeks ago, when she overheard her parents whispering about her step uncles, Jasper and Junior, she called Gunner. Based on what she'd overheard, she was concerned that the Barneses were up to something—like car stealing and car stripping—that might damage Gill's chance of getting a basketball scholarship to Duke. She told him Duke was as picky about a player's character as his athletic ability and didn't want her little brother to miss out because of his family connections—even though the two families weren't close and didn't want to be."

She stopped at the door.

"I think she had hoped the step uncles weren't involved, but if they were involved, she could help Gunner clear up the case against them, and it would be out of the papers and ancient history by the time Gill was a senior."

She slipped into her coat and opened the steel backdoor to a black sky and a drizzle of rain lit by the tall gas-station light beside the building.

I stepped out, snugged my cap, and pulled up the collar on my windbreaker.

As we walked to our car, she said, "While you were gone, I did more digging into Dan's files. On our way to the hospital, I'll tell you what I found out about Looper 'Rabbit' Heister and his boys."

She grinned. "As you and Charlie would say, 'The plot thickens.'"

Chapter 13

DANCING WITH CLUES

B y the time we flew by the Barneses' farm buildings, the rain had stopped, so we got a good look at his red pickup and a black sedan in their front yard. That was it for transportation. We pressed on toward Pinehurst and the Moore County Hospital.

At the hospital, there was good news: Detective Lewis had been moved to a private room. Mom was allowed a brief visit to his bedside. Later, after she'd dried her eyes and we were on our way to the cottage he rented behind the Mannerly house, Mom told me he was semi-conscious but had amnesia and didn't remember what had happened to him.

"Plus," she said, "his jaw is wired shut, so even when he regains full consciousness, he won't be able to talk."

She also said his nurse told her not to worry. He was young and strong, and the prognosis was good. I didn't know what *prognosis* was, but the nurse said it was good, so that's all I needed to know.

Mom also told me what she'd found in the files about the Barneses and the Heisters. It didn't seem that significant to me at the time. I still thought Miss Tuley was the killer with her lethal hands and in her blue car, especially if the murder and the attempted murder were connected, but Mom had ruled her out. Woman's intuition again.

Mrs. Mannerly, a short, plump widow in her eighties, bundled herself up in a wool coat and hat and led us to Lewis's cottage. On the short walk, she wanted to know everything about her renter and what had happened to him. Mom had to speak up, but she answered her questions until we stepped inside the door and Mom froze in midsentence.

The place looked like a tornado had passed through it—overturned furniture and lamps, drawers pulled from a dresser and the contents dumped on his bed, his bookshelves stripped, and books, games, and photos strewn all over the floor. Mom and I looked at each other and read each other's thoughts: *Someone else was looking for his notes.*

Mrs. Mannerly put her hands to her face.

"Oh, my, would you look at this mess?" She looked up at Mom through her wire-framed bifocals. "He's such a nice young man, but mercy...I thought he would be neater than this."

Mom looked at me.

"Whoever did this either found what we're looking for or didn't, but I don't think we could do a better job of searching for it than they did. You ready to go?"

"Yes, ma'am, but first..."

I turned to Mrs. Mannerly and spoke up.

"Mrs. Mannerly, did you see anyone approach this cottage

today or this evening? Did you hear anything or see anything? A car, maybe?"

She cupped her ear. "Did I see anything?"

I spoke a little louder.

"Yes, ma'am. Did you hear or see anything on your property today?"

"Why, no, sweetie. I don't remember seeing or hearing anyone at all on my property today. Except the mailman, of course—Mr. Pickles. He's such a sweet man—always brings my mail to the door and knocks to check up on me."

Mom grinned.

Again, in a loud voice, I said, "Mrs. Mannerly, did Detective Lewis ever leave anything with you, maybe something he wanted you to take care of for him? Especially lately."

She put her soft hand to her rosy cheek.

"Why, no, sweetie. I don't recall him leaving anything with me except a check for his rent. He was very punctual about that."

She looked back into the room and shook her head.

"I just, I just never imagined he would be so messy."

We thanked her and headed back to the SPPD, where Mom opened the front door for me. I retrieved my bicycle and stuffed it in the trunk of the car.

Seated in the passenger seat on the way home, I said, "What were you grinning about back there when Mrs. Mannerly mentioned her mailman?"

She chuckled. "Oh, she's such a sweetheart. Dan just loves her. But the mailman's name is Nickles, not Pickles. She heard it wrong the first time, so to her, he's been Mr. Pickles for the past ten years or more." She smiled. "And he just goes along with it."

After I got home, I went straight to the kitchen cupboard to get a can of Friskies dog food. The rain had stopped long ago, so when I took Superman his food, I wore my ball cap and windbreaker against the cool breeze. I placed his bowl on his sundeck, and he scoffed it up, almost inhaled it. Mammy would not have approved of that dog's dining manners. After he'd finished his business and I had him on his back for a chest rub, I remembered the dance and Chipper's promise of information on the case.

I had something to tell her, too, mainly about the Barneses and Heisters, but I wasn't sure if telling her would break a promise. Sometimes I had trouble remembering what I'd promised and what I hadn't. I decided to wait and play it by ear. That was my usual modus operandi, or MO, as they say on *Dragnet*, and most of the time, it worked for me.

Back inside, and after a quick Swanson's roast beef and mashed potatoes TV dinner with green peas, which was Becky's idea of a complete meal, I showered and dressed for the dance.

The Highland Park Country Club sat on the crest of a low hill above Southern Pines like a long, white country estate for some eastern railroad tycoon—two stories, tall columns, wrap-around porches, and a slate, peaked roof with large dormers. Charlie's dad was a member and played golf there, so I'd been there with Charlie before, but that was for lunch. It was even more impressive at night and decorated for Christmas. The ten-foot Christmas tree in the right corner of the lobby glistened and sparkled with lights and ornaments like an arts-and-crafts work of art.

As we walked through the lobby, each in slacks with a blue sport coat and tie (Charlie's Santa tie a tad more colorful than my green plaid one), Charlie nodded toward the tree.

"That's a Fraser fir from a farm up north. Don't go looking for bodies in it, okay?"

"No problem. I haven't looked for bodies in trees in, oh… almost a week now."

I nodded at a cluster of Girl Scouts gathered at double doors on the right side of the room.

"Ballroom that way?"

"Yep, the scene of the crime. Look at 'em, gathered around like a flock of vultures."

"Let's go over there by the fireplace and leather sofas. I see Big Fry and Jimmy. And hey, how's that pneumonia problem coming along?"

He took another look at the girls and took a deep breath.

"It's getting worse by the minute."

Just as we walked up to Big Fry and Jimmy, both in blue suits and ties, a band started playing Glenn Miller's "In The Mood" from the ballroom. Thanks to Mom's record collection, I had extensive knowledge of the big band era and loved it.

Big Fry pushed his horn-rimmed glasses against his face and stood tall. He looked over Jimmy's head.

"Well, sports fans, it's show time."

Jimmy wrung his hands.

"Let's, let's don't go yet. Let's wait a minute."

Big Fry grabbed him by the sleeve of his suit coat and led him toward the ballroom.

"We're going now, Jimmy, and when I say 'Dance,' you go to Molly and ask her to dance. Got it?" Monty turned his head and winked at us.

"Well, well, sure, Monty. I intend to."

"I know you do."

On our way to the ballroom, Billy Westly, a.k.a. Howdy Doody, came out of nowhere (probably the men's room) and joined us. A group of other boys followed us, probably fifth graders.

As the girls filed into the ballroom, I saw Susie Wilkerson turn to Chipper and smile. It looked like she said something about Charlie. Chipper chuckled and looked back at us.

Oh, that ballroom was something else—crystal chandeliers, garland, and greenery hung from every window, red and gold balls on greenery laid along the mantels above the fireplaces on either end of the room, and a hardwood dance floor in the middle of the room before a large band. And the band, dressed in red sport coats and ties, looked like something I'd seen in the movies, like a Benny Goodman or Glenn Miller band. And they played "In the Mood" like the Glenn Miller band. They "jumped," as my mother would say. I elbowed Charlie.

"I don't think we'll hear any rock and roll tonight, Black Dog—no Chuck Berry or Jerry Lee Lewis from these guys."

"You're probably right. Just as well, though. I still trip over that stupid bop step."

The girls flowed toward the tall windows to the right side

of the room. We hung a left for the tables with the punch bowl and snacks, and the other guys followed us.

Mom had briefed me well.

"Just talk to her first, Nate," she'd said. "Maybe invite her for a cup of punch at the punch bowl. If I know those Girl Scout mothers, they're bound to have a punch bowl."

Actually, they had two punch bowls—one on each end of a long stretch of joined tables with white tablecloths. Between the punch bowls were plates and bowls of fruit and snacks like chips, pretzels, chocolates, and tiny little sandwiches without crusts.

Charlie nodded at the table and smiled.

"This little soirée might not be so bad after all."

"Soirée, Charlie? Soirée? Really?"

"Means party—an evening party, to be exact. Lighten up, Kemosabe. Just follow my lead."

His lead led us straight to the sandwiches, which was fine with me. That TV dinner was history. We took a glass plate from the stack and piled on the sandwiches, cookies, and chips. Charlie had the punch bowl ladle full of punch when we both got a whiff of girl and turned.

"Hi, boys. Buy me a drink?" Chipper, wearing a red-and-white dress with a white lace collar and puffy short sleeves, stood behind us with her hands behind her back.

I grabbed a glass cup, held it over the bowl, and looked at Charlie, who still held the ladle.

"A drink for the lady, barkeep."

Charlie grinned. "Hi, Mary Elizabeth. You want a slice of

orange in yours? I'm not sure what else is in this brew, but it looks like cranberry juice."

"My sources say it's cranberry, orange, and ginger ale with some cinnamon—those sticks floating around in there with the orange slices. Just half a cup and no orange slice, please."

After he poured her punch, she leaned in closer.

"Okay, Charlie, are you going to ask Susie to dance or what?"

He glanced over at the gaggle of girls along the windows.

"Yeah…maybe…in time, but not yet." He looked at me.

"I think Nate wants to talk about the case first. He said on the way over here that you had some information for us."

"After that, will you dance with her?"

"Ah, sure. I guess so." He smiled. "If you'll dance with me."

She winked at me and looked back at Charlie.

"Only after you dance with her."

I elbowed him. "Told ya." I nodded to a leather sofa with a coffee table in front of it.

"Let's go sit over there." I looked at Chipper. "Want to get a plate?"

"No, thanks." She held up her cup. This'll do for now."

Seated on the leather sofa, Chipper between us, we set our cups and plates down before a display of pine boughs with pine cones and gold Christmas balls. Chipper turned to me.

"Nate, how's Detective Lewis?"

I had a bite of chicken salad sandwich in my mouth, so I just gave her a thumbs-up.

"Have you talked with him?"

I shook my head.

"Has he said anything, like what happened and if he saw who did it?"

I swallowed.

"He's just recovered some consciousness and can't talk yet—jaw wired shut. Plus, he has amnesia. I think that means he doesn't remember anything. Mom's gone back tonight to be with him and talk to him. The nurse told her in cases like this, it helps if he keeps hearing a voice he knows and likes."

Charlie scoffed. "That would rule out Chief McDonald."

"Yeah." I looked at Chipper. "So, what do you have for us?"

From across the room, the band played a slow tune I didn't recognize. Monty led Jimmy away from the food and toward the girls, where Molly waited in a white dress with red ribbons in her blonde ponytail. Jimmy rubbed his head.

Chipper nodded toward a group of younger girls who looked like fifth graders.

"See the tall girl in the green-and-white dress with green ribbons in her hair?"

We nodded.

"That's Patty Turner, Rachel and Gill's little sister."

She nodded toward an adult couple who had just stepped onto the dance floor.

"That's their parents, and they're chaperoning tonight."

I recognized the parents, an average-sized man with dark hair and a tall woman with auburn hair, as the couple in the woods with Rachel at the funeral.

I said, "Patty's mother is a Barnes, right?"

"Patty's mother, Edna, is the only child from Mr. Buster's first marriage. That marriage lasted less than a year, then

Edna's mother ran away with Edna, got a divorce, and never remarried. Buster remarried, and that wife was Junior and Jasper's mother. Edna grew up and married Luther Turner, and they had Rachel, Gill, and Patty."

"Geez. So...that makes Buster Barnes Patty's...grandfather?"

"Yes, on her mother's side, and Junior and Jasper are her step uncles."

Charlie swallowed another bite of a tuna fish sandwich.

"Then she has Barnes blood, but not much."

"Not much, and none that they're proud of, but enough to make Rachel, Gill, and Patty taller than average."

Charlie scoffed. "Much taller than average. That Patty is as tall as I am." He plucked another sugar cookie from his plate. "But cute."

"Yes, she is, but so is Susie. You better get over there and go to work, Charlie."

He stuffed the cookie in his mouth and chewed like he didn't hear her. The tune ended, and he swallowed.

"Oops, too late."

He stood with his cup and walked away toward the punch.

I said, "All right, Mary Elizabeth, what's the latest from Patty?"

She finished a sip of punch and cleared her throat.

"The Barneses are up to something. It involves cars, and it's probably not legal. That's all she knows."

She dabbed her mouth with a red-and-white Christmas napkin.

"But she also told me something about Gill. Didn't you tell me one time that your sister is interested in Gill?"

"Yeah, she's all ga-ga-goo-goo over that guy."

"Well, she needn't bother. Gill has the hots for Carol Sue Todd, the cheerleader, and has been after her the entire school year. Sophomore. You know her?"

"Know of her, seen her, but never met her."

"Patty says Carol Sue is dating the student body president. He drives a Buick convertible, and his dad is president of the Bank of Southern Pines. Patty laughs about it. Says her poor brother Gill has been working and saving his money to buy a car, like that will win her over, but with a car or without a car, he doesn't have a chance."

"That's too bad. Gill seems like a nice guy. But I never thought Becky had a shot with him anyhow. An eighth grader with the high school all-American jock? No way."

"Agree. Okay, Nate. You said in the hardware store you had something for me. Give."

I hesitated. In the files Mom had pulled from Detective Lewis's drawer, she found notes he hadn't asked her to type yet. According to the notes, Looper Heister and his boys were back in the bootlegging business and learning how to expand their sales to other counties by working with Buster Barnes. I wondered if "working with" meant learning how to drive fast. I decided not to let that cat completely out of the bag just yet.

"Well, Mary Elizabeth, apparently there is some bootlegging activity going on, and the people involved might not have appreciated the attention they were getting from Officer Lum."

"Names?"

I crossed my fingers behind my back.

"Mom didn't mention names, but you and I already know that Looper Heister has been in the bootlegging business before, so I guess he's one of those people she referred to."

The band started playing "A String of Pearls," another Glenn Miller tune I recognized and something Charlie could dance to—if he wanted to.

I stood. We'd had punch, we'd talked, so I had checked all the boxes. It was time for action. I held out my hand.

"Would you like to dance?"

If I remember anything from my first dance, it was how patient Chipper was with me. She didn't try to correct or critique. She just laughed with me when I laughed at myself, and by the end of the tune, we'd smoothed out my awkwardness, and we were flowing with the music. I always appreciated that about Mary Elizabeth Chippenvale. She just accepted me and didn't critique or blame me—not even when I accidentally scuffed her good shoes, which I later learned were Mary Jane dress shoes.

During the last ten seconds of the tune, Charlie and Susie danced by. He looked at me with a wrinkled brow and tight lips.

Later, because no one else had asked her, I asked Patty to dance. While we danced, I said, "Patty, do you know why Rachel was seeing Officer Lum?"

She pulled back a bit. "Yes."

"So do I, but I haven't told anyone."

She let out a relaxing breath.

"Oh, thank you, Nate. Please don't tell anyone. I've been so worried about her. She has taken his death so personally like it was her fault."

"Well, I think I know for sure that it wasn't her fault."

"May I tell her that?"

"Yes, please do. All Rachel was doing was trying to help Gill, and as far as I know, she didn't do anything that led to Officer Lum's death."

"Yeah, that's what she told me. She was trying to help Gill."

Behind her, Charlie danced by with Chipper and shot me a Cheshire cat grin.

Patty danced a little closer. "Nate?"

"Yeah."

"I think I know what my step uncles are up to."

"Really? Speak to me."

"You know my grandfather used to build and race stock cars, right?"

"I've heard that, yeah."

"Well, thanks to listening to one of my mother's phone conversations, I just found out today that he and his boys are running a school for people who want to learn how to drive fast. He calls it the Barnes Speed School. They even modify the student's cars so they can go faster."

"He's training stock car drivers?"

"He's training anyone, stock car driver or not."

"Anyone we know?"

"No one I know, but I heard the name Urdenbach mentioned."

"Mr. Urdenbach drove for Buster Barnes back in the day, so maybe he's one of his instructors."

"Yeah, that could be."

And, if it paid enough, he could also be the guy that ran Lewis off the road and tried to kill him.

The tune ended, and I walked Patty back to the girl's side of the room. On the way, she said, "By the way, did you know Gill wanted to buy Officer Lum's car?"

I hooked her arm, and we stopped.

"No, I didn't."

"Yeah, Officer Lum was going to show it to Gill, and they were going to talk about it after the game last Friday night. Gill is determined to get a car, you know. He's so in love with Carol Sue Todd that he can't see straight. He thinks a hot car is the answer."

When I returned to the punch bowl, Charlie was reloading his plate, and Chipper was talking with Molly and Jimmy. She saw me and stepped over to me.

"Learn anything from Patty?"

"Nothing that changes anything. The Barneses are into cars. Gill's in love with Carol Sue, so I guess the only news is Gill was interested in Officer Lum's car."

"He was selling his car?"

"Yeah."

I looked for Big Fry.

"I want to talk with Monty. Maybe he's learned more from his cousin, the one who lives out by Looper Heister's place."

Chapter 14

BAD-TEMPERED BLOOD

M onty had not talked with his cousin again, but he agreed to help me look for a phone and call him. We left the party for the lobby area.

A thin old security guy in a blue uniform and a blue tie sat at the desk in the lobby. After we asked if we could use the black phone on his desk, he tapped the phone and said, "All yours, boys." He winked. "As long as it's not long-distance."

I whispered to Monty, "Is Carthage long-distance?"

"No, young man, it's not." The man smiled. "I'm old but not deaf."

"Oh, well, thank you, sir. Sorry."

Monty dialed. It rang, but it rang so long I thought Monty would hang up. Then, "Caleb…? Yeah, Monty…Can you talk?…Okay, I'll be quick. Was anything happening at the Heisters' Wednesday night?" Monty looked at me and shook his head. "Nothing, huh?"

I held up my hand.

"Ask if he's seen a blue Ford sedan over there recently, say in the last week."

"Have you seen any strange cars over there in the last week, like a blue Ford sedan?" He looked at me and shook his head again. "Okay, see you tomorrow night at Granny's...Yeah, we're bringing the rolls and green bean casserole...Okay, bye."

The security man looked up. "Is Rabbit in trouble again?"

Monty looked at me, and I looked at the man.

"Not that we know of, sir. We're just looking for a friend of ours who drives a blue Ford and hasn't been seen since Wednesday night."

"I saw a blue Ford Wednesday night, fairly late too, out on Shelton Road. Looked like there had been a wreck, and the Ford had stopped to look it over."

Whoa. "Did anyone get out of the Ford?"

"Ah...I don't think so. Seems as soon as they saw me coming, they did a quick turn and took off ahead of me. And fast too. That was a fast car. Could that have been your friend?"

"Maybe. He's nosey and likes to drive fast."

"Well, I hope you find him."

"Thank you, sir. Ah, sir, did you happen to stop at the wreck?"

"No, son, I didn't. I was late getting home from our Wednesday night poker game, and my wife worries when I'm late, so I kept going. Not proud of that. I later heard there was a police officer in the wreck, and he wasn't found until daylight." He shook his head.

"No, sir, I'm not proud of that at all."

"I think the officer is recovering okay, sir, so..."

"Oh? Glad to hear it. Thanks for telling me. When he's

back on the force, I'd like to visit with him and apologize. I sure would."

Back in the ballroom, the band played another slow tune. We found Charlie at the punch bowl and Chipper on the dance floor with Billy Westley, who wore a suit and white shirt with one of those cowboy string ties. Monty left me and walked toward the girls like he would ask someone to dance.

I stopped beside Charlie.

"I'm going to get my cup and plate, so don't go away. Got some news on the wreck scene."

Once we were back on the sofa with full plates and cups, Rose danced by with some boy who looked older than us, probably one of her military school beaux. Behind them, Monty danced with tall Donna—good-looking couple. I turned to Charlie.

"Monty called his cousin—nothing, but as it turns out, the security guy who let us use his phone overheard the conversation. He told us about seeing a blue Ford at the scene of the wreck Wednesday night. He said he didn't think the driver got out of the car. The car just turned around and left, and it left in a hurry."

"Well, that must have been whoever ran him off the road, but we found what we were looking for, right?

"Not everything. We're still missing the file Lewis had on the Lum murder."

"Wasn't that his journal you found?"

"No, that turned out to be Lum's journal."

"Oh crap. So, where's Lewis's journal or file or whatever?"

"Good question. It wasn't in his office or the cottage he rented, and he can't tell us yet."

"Not in the car, not in his office, not in his cottage, not with him in the hospital. Somebody stole it."

"Looks that way."

The party ended at ten o'clock, but not before I got the last dance with Chipper and Charlie finished off the last of the ham-salad sandwiches.

Mrs. Shonkasabe drove me home in their Chrysler station wagon and smiled when I told her how popular Charlie was with the girls. She stopped in our driveway and turned to look back at us.

"Charlie, your dad will drive you boys to the game tomorrow night, but he can only stay for the first half. We've got a Christmas party at the Chippenvales'. Then, Charlie, you walk home with Nate, and we'll pick you up after the party."

Charlie nodded. "Yes, ma'am. No problem."

She looked at me and then back at Charlie.

"Your dad's looking forward to the game with you boys, but don't let him stuff himself with junk food, okay? He's gained some weight lately, and that's not healthy."

I opened my backdoor.

"I'll leave that up to Charlie, Mrs. Shonkasabe."

She pointed at Charlie. "Charlie. *Bonne nourriture* only."

"Yes, ma'am, good food only."

She turned around and put her hands on the wheel.

Charlie looked at me with a shrug that said, *I'm going to tell my father what he can and can't eat? Not likely.*

The next day, Friday, December 23, was bright, chilly, and

full of promise. I was only two days and a wake-up away from my first BB gun—a powerful pump BB gun at that. And as a morning bonus, my route had gone without incident. That was a surprise because one of my customers had added a full-grown German shepherd to their family a week ago. That dog had already decided their home was his castle, and he would not allow entry to anyone not in the family. By that Friday, he was no longer confused about who was in his family and who wasn't. Nathan Hawke, the kid on the bicycle who threw things at his house, was definitely not family. He wasn't on the porch that morning, so I tossed the paper and fled.

Another positive note to add to that beautiful sunny morning concerned Detective Lewis. Mom had come home the night before with a smile and the news that Lewis was fully conscious. His nurse had told Mom that Mom's voice and hand-holding had turned the tide for his recovery. Unfortunately, with his jaw wired shut, he still hadn't said anything, and he still couldn't remember what had happened to him. In fact, he couldn't remember anything from the past week, including Officer Lum's murder.

Mom had asked him to write down his last memory, and he wrote, *Returning to Southern Pines with Gunner after a meeting in Raleigh with Abe Bullard.* Then he wrote, *Did Abe ever join SPPD?*

When Mom said, "Yes, he did," he wrote, *Do you know what we planned to do?*

Mom nodded.

He wrote, *How did it go?*

And that's when she had to tell him about Officer Lum's murder.

Mom said he choked up after that news and didn't look up for a long time. She waited patiently, then he wrote, *I really liked Gunner. I'll get his murderer. Count on it.*

Mom said, "I'm sure you will," and then, "Who would do that? Who do you suspect?"

He wrote *I don't remember.*

When Mom left for the night, the nurse walked her to the receiving desk and said, "He's coming back faster than others I've seen. Keep coming to see him. It won't take long."

I went over that information from the night before while I was in the backyard taking care of Superman. That's when I remembered I had Lewis's appointment book. When I went back inside, it was six forty-five. Mom was already up and in the shower, and Granddaddy was fixing breakfast.

After breakfast and while Mom was in a hurry to get to work and didn't have time to question me, I walked her to the car and handed the appointment book to her.

"Detective Lewis's appointment book, Mom. I think if you read this to him, it may help him remember where his notes are, and it might also help him remember if Miss Tuley had a motive. And if she had a motive, did she have an alibi."

She opened the car door. "Okay, but I won't be able to see him until I get off work this afternoon."

"Will you call me and tell me if it worked—if reading it helped him remember?"

She hugged me. "You bet."

She slipped onto the driver's seat and started the car.

"Gotta boogie." She held up the book. "But tonight, I want to hear how you got this." She smiled. "So, get your story straight."

I grinned.

"Yes, ma'am. It's a good story too."

"I'll bet."

She put the car in reverse. "Oh, Becky is doing chow tonight, but I've told her what to cook and not just to heat another TV dinner. Okay?"

"Thank you!" I gave her a thumbs-up and a smile.

"You're welcome." She looked over her shoulder and accelerated down the driveway.

That night Charlie and his dad were a little late picking me up, but we got to the basketball game just as the team came out of the locker room. Gill led them to their bench, where the cheerleaders jumped up and down and encouraged cheers from the crowd.

Gill got Carol Sue's attention, pulled a set of car keys out of his warm-up jacket, and dangled them at her. She ignored him.

We wove our way up between people to the middle of the first section of wooden, collapsible bleachers and sat in the only open spot large enough for three people. The Aberdeen game in any sport was always a big rivalry, so I wasn't surprised that the gym was packed and loud.

Becky and Skinny Jenny were two of the loudest, but thankfully I saw them screaming from the far end of the bleachers. They were too busy worshipping Gill to notice us.

The tip-off went to Aberdeen, and they scored first on a

quick jump shot. They scored again when one of our guys passed the ball to Gill, but it was intercepted and taken down the court for an easy layup.

One of our guys missed a jump shot on our next possession, and Aberdeen got the rebound. When they got it down the court, Gill, number 10 in blue shorts and a white uniform tank top, stole the ball from an Aberdeen player wearing green and gold and dribbled the length of the court. A tall, slender Aberdeen player with a pimple problem caught up and ran stride for stride with him, but Gill made the layup.

That brought a roar from the crowd around us, including Mr. Shonkasabe.

From our sideline, the three cheerleaders jumped up and yelled, "And the score goes up another notch...*clap-clap*...two more!"

I looked up at the electronic scoreboard on the wall at the other end of the gym, and it recorded the new score as Aberdeen 4, Southern Pines 2.

In making the shot, the pimple guy hit Gill on his right arm. The whistle blew, and play stopped. Gill grimaced and shot the guy a look. At the free-throw line, he rubbed his right shoulder.

I looked at Mr. Shonkasabe. "Is he hurt?"

"He got knocked down last week trying to make a layup and fell on his right shoulder. They rubbed some liniment on him, and he was able to get back in the game. He didn't shoot as well after that, and we lost."

The referee tossed Gill the ball, and the crowd on both sides fell silent. It wasn't good sportsmanship or good manners to try to distract the shooter at the free-throw line. He was allowed to concentrate. Gill made both free throws, so the score went to 4 to 4.

I turned to Mr. Shonkasabe. "I guess the shoulder's better."

He smiled. "And a good thing it is. We need him at a hundred percent tonight to have a chance."

Gill ran back up the court to play defense. He smiled at Carol Sue, but she ignored him again.

Just before halftime, Gill shouldered a guy going for an easy layup. The guy slid out of bounds, across the floor, and banged his knee into the stage wall.

As the guy lay there in pain, Gill got called for a foul, his third. He jumped into the face of the referee, stabbed a finger at him, and yelled, "You're blind! I didn't touch him!"

Gill's coach ran out and pulled him aside, but Gill yelled back at the referee, "I didn't touch him!"

The referee called a technical foul on Gill, and the guy he fouled got to shoot three free throws. He only made one. Gill sat on the bench for the remaining minute of the half.

Mr. Shonkasabe looked at us.

"Gill's temper is his worst enemy, boys. He mouthed off at the referee last week too. Too bad, really. He could be a superstar if he could just control that temper." He stood. "I'll come and get you at Nate's, Charlie."

He took a step down between the couples in front of us, said, "Excuse me," and then turned to look back at Charlie. "Don't eat them out of house and home while you're there."

After halftime, Aberdeen extended their lead on two straight buckets by the pimple guy.

Our guys got close a few times in the second half but couldn't get the lead. Then, with ten seconds to go in the game and the score 42 to 41, the pimple guy stole the ball from Gill and took off down the sidelines for the goal that would ice the game.

The crowd stood, and the people around us shouted, "Stop him!"

In desperation, Gill caught up with him and stole the ball back. He turned—dribbling the ball—and ran toward his own goal. He wove between two Aberdeen players, dodged another, then, with one second left, launched a jump shot from the top of the key that dropped into the net at the buzzer—Aberdeen 42, Southern Pines 43.

Charlie and I and everyone around us jumped up and screamed.

On the court, Gill stabbed two fingers in the air and shouted, "Two!"

I stopped yelling and stared at Gill and the chaos on the floor.

Two fingers. Anger. Car.

I grabbed Charlie.

"Charlie, two fingers!"

"Yeah, he does that. It's kinda his signature. When he scores the go-ahead basket or the winning basket, he raises two fingers and shouts, 'Two!'"

"He's our guy, Charlie—he killed Lum!"

"What?"

"Yeah, Lum's two fingers were frozen in the same pose Gill

has now. Lum, the basketball fan who never missed a Southern Pines game, was trying to tell us Gill killed him!"

"Ah, come on, Nate."

Below us, the team surrounded Gill, pounded him on his back, and jumped up and down around him. Still smiling and holding up his two fingers, Gill raised his head and looked toward Carol Sue.

While the other cheerleaders jumped around at center court with the team, Carol Sue left for the exit holding the arm of a tall, clean-cut young guy in a sport coat and tie. *No doubt the student body president with the Buick convertible.*

Gill pushed everyone aside and stomped off for the locker room.

"I'm tellin' ya, Charlie, Gill killed Lum! Look…He had motive—Lum's car to impress Carol Sue. He had opportunity—Lum stayed behind after the basketball game last Friday night, the night he was killed. And he had means—strong hands, Charlie!"

"Yeah, but—"

"And liniment! I smelled liniment at the crime scene. Now, that could have been from Lum, who was using it on his sore muscles, or it could have come from Gill handling the body and blanket—Gill had liniment on him after the game last week."

"Yeah, all that makes sense, Nate, but—"

"You bet it makes sense. I'm afraid Gill has as much of that Barnes bad-tempered blood in him as Jasper or any other Barnes."

"So, what do we do?"

"You go to the pay phone in the hall and call Chief Mc-Donald—he's in the book. Get him or Officer Bullard on the phone and get them over here."

I reached into the pocket of my jeans.

"Here's a nickel."

He took it.

"What are you going to do? Nothing stupid, I hope."

"I'm just going to strike up a conversation with him, just enough to delay him until the cavalry gets here."

The stands had emptied, so I stepped down to the next bench, and Charlie stepped down with me. He grabbed my windbreaker.

"Nate. You just saw what kind of mood he's in, so don't do this. You make the call, and we'll both wait for the cavalry."

I squeezed my lips together.

"Look, I figure whoever killed Lum also tried to kill Lewis. Lewis still has amnesia and can't remember what happened to him, right? So, if the killer is from around here, and I have no doubt that he or she is, then the killer is bound to have connections in the hospital and would know it's only a matter of time before Lewis's memory comes back. They can't afford his memory to come back, so why wouldn't they try to kill Lewis again?"

I held up a finger and shook it at him. "See? Time is a factor here."

"Maybe, but I still don't think you need to do this."

"I'll be fine. A conversation—what's the harm?"

I made a shooing motion with my hands.

"Go, go. I've got to get out back where he'll exit."

Chapter 15

WAR WHOOP

Behind the gym was a small parking lot for coaches, players, and officials lit by a single gas-station light above the exit from the locker room. One row faced the gym, and the other faced the woods. A bright-red Ford sedan with yellow flames painted from the front wheel well to the edge of the driver's door sat in the first space facing the woods. The Ford had a long radio antenna, new black walls, and a dual exhaust. I only had to do one thing to confirm that it was Lum's car with a new paint job and tires.

The two referees and the scorekeeper had already walked to their cars. I stood behind the corner of the gym and watched them drive off.

A few minutes later, a bunch of players came out in jeans, caps, and jackets. In most cases, they wore blue varsity jackets with leather sleeves and a big *SP* embroidered on the front. After they left, only two cars remained—the red Ford and an old black Dodge.

I looked behind me. The front parking lot was empty, at least the part I could see.

The exit door squeaked, and I heard voices. I turned and watched Coach Watts and Gill step onto the concrete stoop and stop. Both wore varsity jackets.

Coach Watts, who was even taller than Gill, snugged his fedora, locked the door, then turned to Gill and pointed at him.

"One more, Gill. That's it. One more flare-up with referees like tonight, and you will watch the next game from the stands. Got it?"

"Yeah, yeah, I got it."

"What?"

"I mean, yes, sir, I understand."

"Goodnight." Watts turned for the black Dodge.

Gill watched him start the car and drive off. Then he picked up a rock in the parking lot, yelled, "Dammit!" and threw it at the biggest pine tree on the edge of the woods. It hit the tree with a crack, and a chip of pine bark flew into the darkness. Head down, he walked toward the red Ford.

I looked behind me. Still no SPPD, no Charlie. I swallowed and walked toward Gill.

As I left the light from the gas-station fixture over the exit, Gill opened the car door and turned.

"Who's there?"

"Hi, Gill. Nathan Hawke, Becky's brother."

"Oh yeah, the liar."

"I've put that unfortunate reputation behind me, Gill. I speak with straight tongue now."

"Yeah, I'll bet you do. Get outta here, kid. I'm going home."

"Great game, Gill. Winning shot. Gotta feel good about

that, so why go home? I'll bet the crowd at the soda shop is waiting for you."

He hung his head. "Look, what do you want? Autograph? What?"

I leaned against the back wheel well and crossed my arms. "Oh, nothing, really. Just wanted to say, 'Good game.'"

"Okay, you've said it. Now get lost."

He slid onto the driver's seat and put the key in the ignition.

I stepped up inside the door before he could close it. I put my hand on the window frame.

"Cool car, man. Mind if I look at the interior?"

Navy-blue color, cloth seat covers—just like Lum's.

"Cool. Navy blue. You don't often see that with a red body."

He grabbed my hand and threw it back at me.

"Get outta my face, kid."

"Again, the name's Nate, but this is a cool car, Gill. Look at this."

I reached under the dash and pressed the chrome button I knew was there from the times I'd ridden with Officer Lum.

From under the hood, a bugle blew, "Charge!"

Lum had been in the armored cavalry and loved that cavalry charge horn.

Gill slammed his hands on the top of the steering wheel.

"That's it!"

He grabbed my jacket, pushed me out of his way, and jumped out of the car. He dragged me a couple of steps and threw me against a pine tree.

"Now, get out of here before I kill you too!" His jaw dropped. "Oh, crap."

I slipped his grasp and turned to run for the front parking lot, but he cut me off and grabbed at me. I dodged his grasp.

He cut me off again. He crouched and stalked toward me.

I backed up.

He lunged at me.

I dodged him again, but I had to back into his car to do it.

He laughed. "Got ya now, lying Nathan Hawke."

Uh-oh.

I dropped to the asphalt and slid under the car—*time to play rabbit vs. gray owl.*

He dropped to his knees and grabbed at me, but I slid toward the passenger side.

He ran to that side, but I slid back to the driver's side.

He ran toward that side.

I slid back, but he faked me out and was back on the passenger side, hiding behind the rear wheel when I got there.

He dropped flat.

I spun around to escape, but he grabbed my left Converse high-top and held it tight.

"Now, you've pissed me off, Nathan Hawke, and you're gonna be sorry."

He had me halfway out from under the car when I heard an Indian war whoop, a *thump*, and Gill let go. I heard grunts and groans and looked up, but from under the car, I couldn't see anyone.

I slid out from under the passenger side, jumped to my feet, and saw two guys rolling around on the edge of the woods, grunting and groaning—Charlie! But Charlie was on the bottom. I ran three steps and leaped.

As I flopped onto Gill, I hooked his right arm.

My momentum pulled us over on our backs and allowed Charlie to roll out from under him.

Gill punched me in the face with a left jab.

Charlie hooked Gill's left arm and pulled him back.

With all three of us on our backs and Charlie and I each holding an arm, Gill yanked his arms together in a King Kong move and slammed Charlie and me into each other.

Dizzy and bleeding from my nose, I hung on.

Charlie let go and rolled over, holding his head.

Gill jumped to his feet and grabbed the front of my windbreaker.

He lifted me and cocked his right arm.

A shadow figure slammed into Gill with a grunt.

Gill let go and fell with the shadow on top of him and both of them on top of Charlie.

The shadow yelled. "Get his arm!"

I dove at Gill and grabbed his right arm again.

Charlie, who had recovered some, grabbed his left arm again. The four of us lay there panting and sweating. I was the only one bleeding.

Gill yelled, "Get off me!"

Tom Ray raised himself to kneel on top of Gill.

"Shut up, dirtbag." He looked at me.

"What the hell do you think you're doing?"

"I'm...Phew...I'm catching a murderer."

Charlie looked up and blew a pine needle out of his face.

"*We're* catching a murderer!"

Tom Ray shook his head. "Don't we have SPPD for that?"

"Sometimes," I said. "What are you doing here?" I grinned. "Not that I'm disappointed, you understand, but I thought you'd moved."

"Change of plans, but I'm here kneeling on this dirtbag's chest because you people were disturbing the thinking space around my thinking tree."

He nodded to a tall magnolia tree at the corner of the woods, and then he took a handkerchief from his coat pocket.

"Here. Wipe your nose." He handed it to me. "And by the way, Nate—"

The scene suddenly lit up with a spotlight and car lights from an approaching car. The driver seemed to take a few seconds to spot us, then the car accelerated across the front parking lot and stopped perpendicular to Gill's red car with the spotlight on us.

Officer Bullard rested his arm on the open window frame of the cruiser and smiled.

"Looks like I'm late to the party. Be right there."

He put the car in neutral, opened the door, and then stepped out with handcuffs in hand.

The three of us stood, and Bullard cuffed Gill. He put him in the cruiser's backseat, took the keys to Gill's car, locked it up, then turned.

"We'll be back to impound this later."

I lightly punched Charlie. "So, you called SPPD after all. I'd given up on you."

He pushed his hair back over his ears.

"You had reason to give up. First, I had to wait while a couple of giggly girls called for a ride home, then I called the SPPD office, then I called Chief McDonald, then finally just threw up my hands. Nobody answered!"

I looked at Officer Bullard. "Then how did you get the call?"

Bullard slid behind the wheel and closed the door. He handed me a tissue from a box on the seat.

"Your mom can explain that, Nate. Got to go now. Merry Christmas!"

He drove off with the next SPPD inmate with Barnes blood slumped in the backseat.

A few minutes later, after I'd plugged my bloody nose with the tissue he'd given me, the three of us walked up Ridge Street toward Tom Ray's house and the turn to my house on Orchard Road. I shivered and crossed my arms.

Charlie pulled up the collar on his denim jacket.

Tom Ray raised a hand.

"As I was saying before the law arrived…Gill may think he killed Officer Lum, but he did not. Yes, when Lum wouldn't sell his car for less than three hundred dollars and wouldn't take the two hundred and sixty-five Gill had, Gill got pissed and knocked him out with Lum's four-cell shiny chrome flashlight. But that didn't kill him."

"Whoa," I said. "What was Gill doing with Lum's flashlight?"

"Oh, well, let me back up."

He pulled up the collar on his coat.

"I'm in my thinking tree, see? My father had been slapping me around again—you noticed that Saturday morning, right?"

"Yeah, I guessed that."

"I'm in my tree, the game is over, the people have gone home, and I'm trying to figure out how to get me and my mom away from my father—hopefully for good. I hear a car with a loud rumble and look down to see a red Corvette pull into the lot. It backed into the edge of the woods and out of sight.

"The driver gets out of the car and walks over to the last car at the end of the back parking lot—a medium-blue Ford sedan—*ocean blue,* I think they call it. Okay, he gets to the blue Ford, bends down to the left rear tire, and lets the air out. Then he goes back to his car and just sits there.

"A minute or two later, a man walks out from the front of the gym—little guy. He walks toward the back lot, the lot right under my tree."

"Officer Lum."

"That's right."

Charlie leaned in. "They talk money while Lum changes the tire. Gill holds the light. Gill gets ticked and whacks him."

"Exactly. Gill panics and runs around to the gym entrance, where I presume he called somebody. Meanwhile, the guy gets out of the Corvette and jogs over to Lum—a big guy, maybe six two and two hundred pounds. He checks to see if Lum's alive, decides he is, then he strangles him." Still in step with us, Tom Ray looked at me.

"Now he really is dead." He coughed. "I think the guy was there to ambush Lum, and Gill made it easy for him."

I blew out a breath that turned into a mist.

"Wow. Did you recognize the guy?"

"There's only one guy in town who drives a red Corvette. They only came out a year and a half ago."

Charlie held out his hands. "Well?"

"Mr. Rex McAllister, our teacher's husband."

Chapter 16
UNTRAINED AND IMMATURE

In the end, Mr. McAllister was convicted of the murder of Officer Lum and the attempted murder of Detective Lewis. He was driving Lum's car when it ran Lewis into the tree. As a student in the Barnes Speed School, he knew how to drive fast and had access to the car that was there to be modified for Gill. Plus, as the subject of an investigation over embezzlement of funds from the plumbing supply business that led to bankruptcy, he knew he was on Lum's and Lewis's radar. The money he had embezzled and the money he made as the Raleigh theft ring accountant and local contact for the car and bicycle thefts funded his fondness for fast cars like the Corvette. The Pinehurst job turned out to be a part-time job he used to cover his ongoing connection with the Raleigh ring. He was sentenced to life. Mrs. Mac divorced him, stayed at our school, and found a new husband.

Jasper Barnes, who repaired McAllister's tell-tale dents and scrapes from the accident, was convicted of tampering with evidence, accessory to murder for helping Gill dispose of the body in the Frazer fir, and dealing in stolen cars. After he patched and painted Lum's car in time for Gill to use to impress Carol Sue, he sold it to Gill for $200. He did three years in state prison.

Gill was convicted of the assault on Officer Lum and the assault on me, plus car theft. He was the one who put Lum in the trunk and drove the body to the tree farm. But he didn't do any time because he was a minor. He was also guilty of being the car-theft ring connection to bicycle thefts, where he made money for a car. He worked under Mr. McAllister. Gill was sent to a missionary school in the mountains of West Virginia. The last I heard, he was the leading scorer on their basketball team, and he had yet to hear from Duke University.

Tom Ray's mother got a divorce, got the house, and Tom Ray rejoined my paper route. I never had to deal with that German shepherd again.

By the time Mom got home from the hospital that night— the night that became known in our family and Charlie's as the night of "Black Dog's Attack"—Charlie and I had finished off the last of the peanut butter and graham crackers plus a can of Campbell's bean soup.

Mom joined us, and we sat Indian-style beside the Christmas tree and around the fireplace with a cup of hot chocolate and Bing Crosby singing "The Most Wonderful Time of the Year" in the background. Granddaddy sat on the sofa and hummed along with Bing.

At first, Mom was shocked by my swollen and purplish nose, but I assured her I would live and the nose wasn't broken. She didn't believe me, and I had to see the doctor the next day, but…It wasn't broken. At least, not that time, but that's another story.

After Charlie and I told her about our fight with Gill and his threat to kill me, she shot me the evil eye.

"Nathan Benjamin, you promised me no more encounters with murderers. You lied to me."

"No, ma'am. I didn't lie. Gill only thought he'd killed Officer Lum. Mr. McAllister was the real murderer, and I never encountered him."

Before she had time to think that one through, I said, "By the way, Officer Bullard told us you'd explain how he knew to come to our rescue."

She looked at me, her big brown eyes searching mine like they were looking for any signs of deceit.

"Ah, Mom?"

She sighed. "Well, okay. Your idea to read Dan's appointment book to him worked. He kept writing, *clue, clue* like he was trying to remind himself of the connection.

"Finally, after a process of elimination, I said, 'Clue game?' His eyes lit up. I said, 'Your file on Gunner's murder is hidden in the Clue game at your house?' He nodded. I raced to his cottage, found the file, and read why he suspected Gill, Jasper, and Rex McAllister. I called home, and you weren't there, so I called Abe and got him out there to check on you."

She shook her head. "Almost too late."

Charlie pushed his hair back.

"Not really, Mrs. Hawke. We had it under control."

She smiled and touched the knot on his forehead.

"I can tell."

Detective Lewis was at our house for Christmas and Christmas dinner that year, but in his case, it had to come through a straw. Mom did the turkey and dressing plus peas and carrots and loved pampering Lewis. Becky did the sweet potato casserole, and although it killed me not to rag her about choosing another loser boyfriend, I let it go. It was, after all, Christmas.

Granddaddy presented his bookshelves with a beautiful varnish that had dried in time, and I got my Boy Scout canteen and cooking kit.

Unfortunately, the pump BB gun did not appear under the tree that year due to a clause in the unwritten contract Dad had made with Mom—no BB gun for the boy until he's twelve. Thankfully, my birthday was only six months away, but that's another story.

That night, on Superman's deck with him beside me chewing on a stick of beef jerky, I looked up at the stars that covered the sky, some in wide twinkling streaks, and said, "Superman, I'll be twelve this coming year, and you'll be two."

He looked up at me and said, "Hurrum?"

"Yes, me twelve, you two. Time for us to grow up and for you to learn to sit and stay."

He groaned and cocked his head like, *Give it a rest, boss. Being untrained and immature works for me. Why would I want to change?*

I thought about that a minute—being twelve, I mean. One more year to be a kid with minimum responsibilities, like Superman, and one more year of fun things like Little League baseball. I was really looking forward to baseball season. Unless some hotshot kid showed up in the spring, I'd be our first-string shortstop.

Little did I know that a hotshot kid named Cody Kenner would show up, and I would be back in centerfield. But that wasn't all bad. Baseball people say you put your strongest players up the middle—catcher, pitcher, shortstop, centerfielder—so until the day I ran across a corpse out there in the hot sun and tall grass of Memorial Park, I enjoyed playing centerfield. I did not necessarily enjoy Cody Kenner and his possible connection to that corpse, but that's another story. I'll tell you that story and cover the family drama that went with it in book three, *The Centerfield Corpse*.

Back on Christmas night 1955, out there on Superman's sundeck enjoying his company and the beautiful night sky, I agreed with his sentiment about life: Being untrained and immature wasn't all bad. I smiled and let out a big sigh. For the time being, I could dig it.

ACKNOWLEDGMENTS

I want to thank Julie Epps and Charlotte Ainsworth for their fearless first draft editing and critique, Julie Murphy for her insight into the story and intelligent counsel, and Justin Clark for his website design, technical knowledge, and guidance in the baffling world of computers.

I'd also like to thank my editor, Marcia Ford, for her advice on what makes a novel a good read. Marcia's knowledge of the art and sharp eye made this a better book.

ABOUT THE AUTHOR

Randolph Crew is the author of three novels, including two military action-adventure novels based on his 793 combat missions. He holds an MA degree in counseling from Webster University and a BS degree in Business from Auburn University. Now retired and mellowed (his words), he's having fun writing cozy murder mysteries for ages 10-110. His mysteries take place in Southern Pines, NC, where he lived when he was a junior high student with a reputation. For recreation, he enjoys hiking the great outdoors in his home state of Alabama. You can find him there or on the web at www.rcrewauthor. com. He'd like to hear from you.

Amazon Author:
https://www.amazon.com/author/randolph.crew

Facebook:
https://www.facebook.com/rcrewauthor

Twitter:
https://www.twitter.com/rcrewauthor

Website:
http://www.rcrewauthor.com